GREENHORN GORGE

Fate overtook drifter Danny O'Maldon shortly after he left Boot Hill City with his winnings at cards. A sheriff's posse, following a bunch of bank robbers, latched on to Danny by accident. This misfortune plunged Danny into the affairs of the Circle H ranch, where he became involved with a personable young woman. So, instead of ducking and running, Danny gambled with his very life in clashes with the bank robbers in notorious Greenhorn Gorge . . .

DAVID BINGLEY

◆

GREENHORN GORGE

00634 23345

Complete and Unabridged

LINFORD
Leicester

First published in Great Britain in 1981
under the name of
'Frank Silvester'

First Linford Edition
published 2003

British Library CIP Data

Bingley, David, *1920 –*
  Greenhorn gorge.—Large print ed.—
Linford western library
1. Western stories
2. Large type books
I. Title II. Silvester, Frank, *1920 –*
823.9'14 [F]

ISBN 0–7089–4909–6

Published by
F. A. Thorpe (Publishing)
Anstey, Leicestershire

Set by Words & Graphics Ltd.
Anstey, Leicestershire
Printed and bound in Great Britain by
T. J. International Ltd., Padstow, Cornwall

This book is printed on acid-free paper

1

The ridge was a lush wooded hogsback with an undulating spine, liberally clothed in various species of small oak and pine trees, and additionally draped in thriving fern and other green plants. Beneath the foliage, grass retained a lot of moisture and made a pleasant resting spot for men and animals.

The shallow copse where the muscular dun gelding cropped the tufts was highly placed along the crest. At every short forward movement, the slackened saddle on its back rocked uncertainly and threatened to slip further round its barrel.

The rider was on his knees, happily absorbed in cutting his name into a new leather belt purchased in the nearby town known as Boot Hill City. The fifteen minutes it took to do the knife work seemed longer in the first hour of a sunny afternoon, and yet the fellow was not particularly tired. He rolled a long thin cigar around his lips so that the smoke from it would miss his half-closed light blue eyes, and smiled to himself.

Daniel O'Maldon. The name looked good in the shiny new leather. Something about it matched an optimistic, buoyant mood in himself. He slipped it through the loops in the top of his denim levis and adjusted it about his waist. It felt right. He drank a couple of fingers of whisky from a flat bottle, and chased it down his throat with a swig of lukewarm water from his canteen.

Taking the cigar from his mouth, he yawned hugely and wondered what he could do to amuse himself for a short while before moving on again.

He had shaved early that morning and his neutral-coloured sideburns were neatly trimmed, too. After squinting in a small circular mirror at his regular features and trail clothes, he made a few minor adjustments to his appearance. A grey, flat-crowned stetson came off the close-cropped head, revealing the two-shot Derringer stached inside it, so that the headgear could be dusted and its snakeskin band polished up a little.

Next, he removed the blue bandanna from his neck and hauled the contrasting red shirt off his body. In taking it off, he turned it inside out. His wide mouth quirked into a grin as he removed pasteboard aces from secret pockets in the sleeves.

That very morning, he had used some of those secreted cards to out-cheat two fairly expert card players in a Boot Hill City saloon and he had managed to quit town with his winnings without his own cheating being challenged. Two hundred dollars, mostly in bills. Not bad for a travelling hombre who only relied upon gaming for a part of his income.

In his travels, which had begun three years ago, O'Maldon had often been close to gun-play as a result of his gambling, but somehow or another he had not been involved in any serious shooting. Not that he didn't expect it. It was always possible, in the life of a man who consistently played to win.

Brooding over his way of life prompted him to test his weapons. He stuck the aces in the bark of trees and threw his belt knife at them. His aim was not too bad, and he soon got the hang of how to throw the knife so that the point went into the target.

Soon, however, he tired of that skill, and three times banged off the two shots of his Derringer. He had been warned many times that a Derringer was not a man stopper. It was only effective from a few feet away. So, as his shooting with the miniature weapon was nothing to get excited about, he loaded it, tossed it aside and gave his attention to the .45 Colt which normally hung at his right hip when he wanted to project a tough image.

At a modest range, he began to hit the cards within a dozen shots, but from a few steps further away he was not so good. Frustration was building up in him; and he was wondering what sort of a showing he could give with his Winchester .73 when some distant movement on the trail he had used from town took his attention and made him decide to postpone practice with the rifle.

Instead, he casually replaced his shirt, bandanna and hat and hauled a battered looking spyglass from a saddle pocket. The half-mile distance from the hogsback rapidly dwindled as a tightly grouped bunch of determined riders goaded their mounts to a great effort. The watcher on the ridge studied their progress with great interest. After a few moments of unease, he quite rightly assumed that this bunch could have nothing to do with his own profitable adventures and speedy withdrawal from town.

Were they outlaws or a regular peace officers' posse?

Five minutes later, the riders went out of sight near the end of the ridge.

O'Maldon licked his dry lips and waited for them to show up again on the clearly marked perimeter track which skirted the north side of the ridge. A slight feeling of tension built up in the observer as the time dragged.

A climber had been near enough to be seen for almost a minute when O'Maldon removed his attention from the perimeter track and scanned the fading cloud of dust which had first attracted him. Suddenly he saw the diminutive climbing figure making rapid progress, following the line of the crest.

Toiling for height was a small, swarthy Mexican, his head mostly hidden beneath the brim of a stained steeple hat. The spyglass brought him up close. A flapping black bolero kept pace with the weaving bowed legs. A disembodied voice called out for the climber to hurry. The Mexican paused for a brief rest, knowing his partners could not see him. He then lunged forwards and upwards once again, until

6

he judged himself high enough to do a proper reconnaissance.

O'Maldon felt hot just watching him, and seeing the perspiration stain and spread over the soiled shirt.

Presently, the two watchers were both studying the same dusty section of track which linked their present location with town.

The second cloud of dust eclipsed the first and came closer at the same amazing pace. The Mexican moved first to one side and then the other, his spyglass trained on the cloud, straining to catch a glimpse of the riders making it.

A raucous, impatient voice, sharpened by anger, called up from below. 'Hey, Velasco, you takin' a siesta up there? What's keepin' you, eh?'

'I hear you! I have the posse in sight! They're makin' good speed, as well! I'm on my way down, right now! Don't leave without me! You hear!'

O'Maldon actually heard the Mexican's spyglass fold down. The next time he looked, the small man was almost out of sight, and only a swaying bush or two confirmed his progress as he raced for the lower level, his comrades and his mount.

* ★ ★ ★

United once more, the six impatient riders started to make tracks around the northern side of the great sprawling ridge. Within minutes, the man on the crest observed them with his naked eye. He had them in sight for a while, and he felt cheated when one and all disappeared at the same time. It was almost as if a cave in the side of the ridge had absorbed them.

The approaching posse gradually took over the watcher's attention, and would have held it exclusively had it not been for the voices.

Men called to one another. Voices muted by the walls of the narrow defile through which they were moving seemed strange at first.

'Say, Ringo, ain't we wastin' time,

toilin' up this fault with the posse gainin' ground on us all the time?'

A second voice was also tinged with anxiety. 'I reckon we could have been one helluva lot nearer the ranch if we'd kept right on goin' instead of waitin' for Velasco to exercise his one good eye!'

There was a pause, while O'Maldon strained his ears.

'We ain't goin' directly to the ranch! I thought I told you that before we left town! Now shut up, an' let's ride! I came up here so's the sheriff would run out of trail to follow. It seemed a good notion. I still think it's a good idea, so help me!'

Bobbing heads, and sometimes horses' necks showed where a fault in the rock structure of the hogsback had formed a narrow, scarcely detectable track, just wide enough for a horse and rider to negotiate.

O'Maldon whistled soundlessly, marvelling at the amount of action taking place all around him. Perhaps twice as many deputised riders faded from sight as the first group had done. There was a lot more shouting and milling around, but the posse resumed the chase without much of a pause.

Ringo and his boys were quietly emerging from the fault back onto the main track when the sheriff and his party reined in a little way beyond the other end of the detour, having run out of 'sign' to follow.

Still marvelling at the developments, Danny O'Maldon strayed out onto a bulking outcrop and strained to catch the first glimpse of the milling party of pursuers. A rider who had dismounted in order to check where the renegades had gone looked at the same time and saw the red-shirted figure bringing up a spyglass to observe them.

'Will you take a look up there, sheriff?'

His voice was hoarse and not loud enough to carry to the heights, but his excitement and the promise of his pointing finger caused a sudden outcry.

The attention of each and every man in the posse became focussed on the high ground.

'What? What did you see, Jake?'

'Are they up there? Whereabouts exactly . . . ?'

Before the rest of the group moved into a position to observe the outcrop, the lone watcher had ducked out of sight. He kept well back, leaning against a tree and nervously wondering what would happen next.

'Hold on a second! I'll show you!'

The man in question hauled his rifle out of its scabbard, hastily put it up to his shoulder and blasted off a bullet. The sudden whine of the small projectile and the flying chips of rock as it ricocheted off the edge of the outcrop caused a swift drop in tension.

The riders down below forgot their temporary frustration, joining in with their shoulder weapons and filling the air with gunfire, flying splinters and the unmistakable smell of smoke.

'They're up there, on the ridge,' a

dominant voice yelled. 'They *have* to be up there, on account of the sign runnin' out!'

Another fusillade of bullets probed the position which overlooked them. For a short time, Daniel O'Maldon crouched low, wondering if his Irish luck had turned against him and whether he was due to die through a spent bullet fired in anger at a bunch of men he did not even know.

Gradually it became clear to him that he would have to back off before the furious onslaught of the aggressive town riders who were obviously keen on a blood-letting.

The situation became even more desperate when the secret track in the rock fault was discovered, and the sheriff and deputy headed their party onto the higher ground.

2

Some twenty minutes later, Ringo and his five partners hit a short downgrade track which led into a huge rectangle of cleared ground. Perhaps ten years earlier, a thriving mining company had worked the ground over an acre or two, searching for copper which had at first proved to be there in sufficient quantities for marketing.

As often happened, however, the fairly extensive family which began the work lost interest and moved away to other parts where they hoped the pickings were easier.

All across the great elongated square were rusting rails, heaps of ties, derelict huts and a wagon or two. Enough evidence to interest a drifter or two, but not quite sufficient to prompt anyone to reopen the mine.

As soon as the sweating horses

touched the lower level, the leader held up his hand and checked the others.

'You listenin', boys? After this, keep right in behind me until we make the top left-hand corner of the work area. There, instead of takin' the trail that goes on beyond — '

'The trail to the ranch, Ringo?' a rider boldly interrupted.

Ringo's bulbous hazel eyes appeared to protrude even more as the leader glowered at a slumped over-weight balding rider forking a grey gelding.

'Yer, Raich, that's what I planned to say before you interrupted. At that corner, we all turn right, skirt the rock walls along there, an' go to earth in one of the tunnels. All except Velasco, that is. He stays behind for a while, collects a tree branch with some foliage on it, an' uses that to wipe out our tracks from the corner to the tunnel entrance. You all got that?'

There was a dry-throated chorus in the affirmative. After scanning the direction they had come from, the

14

renegade bunch made the manoeuvre outlined by their boss. Fifty feet into the shadowy gloom of the dank mining tunnel, they dismounted and mopped themselves down, recovering their breath, lighting cigarettes and excitedly discussing the five bags of money which they had carried along with them across their saddles.

The leader suggested the 'take' had been around thirty thousand dollars which would mean a healthy shareout, if all went well. This sobering note started the other four figuring again.

Halberd, a greying lean rider with black barred brows, rocked the saddle of the skewbald which carried him, and peered back towards the entrance.

He remarked: 'Velasco is thorough, all right. It always seems to take him longer to do a job than I figure it, boss. Why do you always use the Mex? I mean, after all, he's only got the one eye. Maybe he ain't the best choice for scoutin' jobs.'

Frenchy Dupont, a black-bearded

former Canadian trapper, screwed up the shapeless stetson he had worn for the raid, stuffed it in his saddle pocket and stuck his favourite fur cap on his head.

'Maybe there's somethin' in what Jake is sayin', boss. On account of all that shootin', I got to wonderin' if the posse spotted Velasco up there on the ridge. What do you think?'

Ringo Hickman hauled off his side-rolled hat and stuck it on his saddle horn between the two money bags hanging there. For a moment, his hard smouldering eyes regarded the stylish brown stetson banded with a pattern of small coins. Then he turned away, tugging at the lobe of one of his long ears. His small cruel features relaxed into a near smile. He ran a hand through his close-cropped fair hair and flapped his black leather vest.

'Boys, Velasco will be here in a minute. He won't lead anyone to us. Okay, so he has only one eye. But he surely knows how to use it, an' this far, since I resumed 'business' in the Panhandle, he's been lucky for me. So relax, will you? All we need, after this, is a modicum of luck, an' a lot of patience.'

Red Vallance, a homely freckled character, with carrot red hair, a lantern jaw and a short upper lip, put a match to a long thin cigar protruding from a gap in his front upper teeth. He found a rock and squatted on it.

'Havin' the sheriff an' a posse ploddin' into town just a few minutes after we'd hit the bank wasn't my idea of good luck, amigos. He ought to have been in the county seat fifteen miles away. It ain't good, deputised riders bein' this close.'

The others scowled at Vallance, but no one chided him for his gloomy remarks. Presently, the sounds of an approaching horse, dragging something, carried to the tense group in the tunnel. Velasco pushed aside the old canvas screen at the entrance and tossed aside the tree branch which he had been using to obliterate their tracks.

'The job's done, boss. I heard tell in town, while I was horse mindin' outside the bank, that a 'breed with a hair-trigger temper had fired a homestead with his employer's family in it last night. That's why the sheriff had a posse on the prowl near Boot Hill. I don't figure they caught the 'breed, though.'

Hickmann nodded and commented. He then picked up the tree branch himself and obscured the horse tracks on either side of the screen.

'We ain't stayin' right there, boys. This maze of tunnels has at least one more exit. You'd be surprised where it leads to. But I ain't tellin' you right now. So we walk the broncs, from here on in.'

Quite unexpectedly, Hickmann produced a lamp from a niche in a rock wall. When it blossomed into light, his partners showed a keenness to move on.

Danny O, as his substitute parents used to call him a few years back, panicked when the bullets started to fly in his direction.

His movements were jerky. He lacked the steadiness of hand which had proved so useful when he was at the card table. And yet he was able to master his nerves, with an effort. Having loaded his gear onto the back of his dun gelding, he took the excited animal by the reins and walked it away from the direction of town.

The bullets had ceased to fly, but it was clear by the occasional shouts that the riders of the posse were making steady progress. As soon as they realised the lesser track did not go all the way to the top, no doubt the lead would start to fly again . . .

Danny O thought he ought to cross over the crest and make his escape by way of the south side, but when he sought to cross he was frustrated by a long series of rock pinnacles, all seemingly attached to one another like the upstanding ridges on a prehistoric monster's back.

He raced along, half-doubled, hauling on the reins, and only succeeded in getting out of breath. The gelding stumbled and further agitated him, so that he changed his mind and instead sought to make his way down the virgin slope above the fault track.

Caution on the part of the gelding kept him from breaking his neck, as ferns, spiked bushes and saplings combined forces with twisted tree roots to bring about his downfall. He came upon the overhang above the concealed track without being aware of it. After teetering on the brink, he lost his balance, slipped over the edge and found himself hanging by the reins with his boots scrabbling against the rough, layered side of the defile.

A feeling of being trapped, coupled with an echo of approaching riders made him want to get back out of the defile as quickly as possible. Eventually, he managed it; his hands were prickled and a small piece of skin parted company with his wrist as the gelding struggled and finally hauled him clear.

After that, he was not so cautious, but a lot of progress was made in a slithering advance parallel with the defile. Several slight scratches emitted blood around his cheeks and jaw, but the lower level came up quite suddenly when he had temporarily lost count of time. Snorting with exertion, the gelding suddenly jumped on bent legs into the fault. It shook itself, rose and pawed the ground, prior to snickering fitfully and showing mild signs of distress.

Gasping with relief, Danny leaped to join it, and eased the metal and leather about its head. Scarcely daring to look back, he mounted up and headed the dun in the direction which the runaways had taken.

The six galloping horses had left their prints in the dust of the old eroded trail, and here and there fresh droppings lent authenticity to the telltale markings. Danny pushed the gelding for over a quarter of a mile. Necessity then made him slow down, and some of the stiffness went out of his back which had become rigid with tension.

The recent markings led quite definitely into the old mine workings, and the lone rider followed them, reasoning that the road agents would probably know better than he did how to dodge the relentless posse.

As he worked his way through the abandoned trappings of the work area, he had time to think about other men and the way they earned a living. For him, cow nursing did not come easy. Neither would mining, he supposed, if he was given the opportunity. He fell to wondering what the miners had done with themselves. Had they moved on, to open up new mines in a different region, or had they abandoned the idea of winning riches from the earth in the form of metal and turned their attention to sod busting or cattle raising?

The north-west corner of the cleared area coincided with harder going under the hoof. Danny failed to notice that the sign was no longer with him as he rode clear of the copper mine and headed north over seemingly unbroken arid country to free himself of pursuit.

Perhaps a mile or a mile and a half went by before the soil re-established itself and began to take on the greenness of coarse grass again. After that, the terrain slowly improved, undulating in gentle switchbacks. Occasional patches of promising green scrub broke up the landscape, eventually being replaced by big bushes and low gnarled trees. The merciless sun, heading relentlessly for the west, made the rider sleepy, so that he almost failed to notice the first small group of longhorn steers away to his left.

Barbed wire appeared without his being aware where it had started. He was on ranch land, and the acreage was vast. He began to entertain notions that he had left the posse behind forever, and the need to come up with a useful story to explain his presence on private ground gave him a useful subject on which to centre his thoughts.

From time to time, he wondered if the renegades were ahead of him, somewhere across the broad range of this formidable cattle spread. If so, how would *they* explain *their* presence when the buildings came up closer and they had to answer a challenge?

With a sudden touch of Irish pessimism, he wondered if the owner of the ranch would treat him in the same way as the posse had done.

3

The Circle H cattle and horse ranch was not only large in size: at any given time it could muster between five and six thousand head of cattle and several score well-bred horses of all types.

Noah Hickmann, the owner, had taken over about eight years previously, buying out the previous owner with an offer of ready money which was less than the real value of the spread; but which enabled the originator of the outfit to move away to Canada at a time when most of his kinsmen were making a bid to have him with them.

Hickmann went to town when he had to, or sent one of his hired hands to collect essential stores, but he had a reputation for being taciturn and difficult to get to know. Some suggested he kept himself to himself because his dark-haired, sallow-complexioned wife probably had traces of Indian blood in her veins. Others were of the opinion that he had raised the money to buy the Circle H by widespread long-term rustling, carried out either in New Mexico territory, or the equally unsettled and vulnerable land to the north of the Texas Panhandle known as the Cherokee Strip.

However he had come by his ready money, Noah Hickmann knew his way around cattle and horses. He had prospered, and his neighbours in Red River County in the Panhandle allowed him his privacy and did not pry too often or too closely into his personal affairs.

The Circle H's lookout system worked well. All the score of fit cowpunchers were trained to be constantly on the alert for strangers and anyone who had no business on the ranch land. Consequently, when a cowpuncher known as Dixie happened to peer out from the upper observation hatch in the top of the spread's windmill and noticed the approach of the stranger on a dun gelding he acted accordingly to prearranged instructions.

Two minutes later, he had emerged from the small door highly placed on the mill, caught hold of a sail, and allowed himself to be carried down to earth in a slow but spectacular fashion.

Dixie was a small man with a nose and chin like Mr Punch; as he hurried through the cluster of buildings, headed for the ranch house, he leaned forward from the hips and gave the impression he was on an errand of great importance.

The smith and his negro striker saw him. Likewise the Chinese cook from his workroom adjacent to the bunk-house. Two sweating hands forking hay in the open-sided barn paused to see what he was up to, and the plump Mexican female housekeeper marked his approach across the rear paddock which had been stippled with stones to prevent it becoming a quagmire in winter.

Dixie danced up the steps onto the rear gallery, knocked on the kitchen door, entered with his big-peaked working cap in his hand and pointed to the door leading through to the front of the house. The housekeeper shrugged hugely, lifting her bosom. A brown-haired girl appeared at another door, saw the intruder and withdrew again.

Dixie moved on, negotiated the internal passage and stepped into the low, roomy living room of the house with a half smile on his face.

'Mr Hickmann, sir, there's a stranger on the way in from the south track. You want anythin' special done about him?'

Noah Hickmann was a stocky character with receding fair hair and baggy grey eyes. Hatless, he looked his forty-seven years, but he wore a big black Texas-rolled stetson even when he was indoors. The low-beamed ceiling made him look bigger than his five-feet nine-inches, making him stoop slightly. He had a perpetual frown on his lined face which was born largely out of a deep-rooted suspicion of his fellow men.

'Is he anybody *you* know, Dixie?'

The owner stood with his hands on his hips, showing a lot of white shirt front above his substantial belt, and sharing his attention between the window and his informer. The small man began to shuffle uncertainly from one foot to the other, and then started to retreat towards the kitchen door.

'Why, no, boss. I just thought you'd like to know in good time, that's all. I — er, I'll get back to work, then.'

Hickman ignored him, giving his full attention to what was happening in the front paddock. Dixie slipped out again, unnoticed.

The rhythmic beating of a hammer on metal in the smithy ceased. Several men thought of intercepting the intruder, knowing the boss was watching and that he was already on the lookout for visitors. The two hay forkers took time in making up their minds, but they were ahead of anyone else, running across the paddock and waiting one on either side of the well-ridden dun gelding and its nervous rider.

'You got business on the Circle H spread, mister?' one asked.

Danny O made a big effort to seem relaxed and to give a reasonable account of himself, even to the hired hands. He rounded out his blue innocent eyes and gave a broad, fetching smile to his interrogators. The flat-crowned stetson was off his head, showing the short brown hair with its auburn highlights when he replied in the negative.

'Nope, can't say I've any business here at all,' he admitted, shaking his head. 'But I sure enough would like to make the acquaintance of the owner, if he has a minute or two to spare. The name's O'Maldon. Will you ask him if he'll see me?'

All the time he was answering, Danny was drying out the band of his stetson with his blue bandanna and watching for covert developments. The two ranch hands hesitated. Hickmann stayed on the watch through the window, and a tall lean individual slipped out of the smithy on long bowed legs to intervene.

Vic Cardine, Hickmann's nephew through his first marriage, acted the part of unofficial *segundo* at the spread when the owner permitted it. He matched Danny for age and weight, but was slightly taller. The hired hands found him sneaky, aggressive and hostile most of the time. He was hatless on this occasion, showing a low bony forehead and dark hair receding at the temples. His green bandanna had been removed from his neck and tied to the braces which supported his levis. His red-and-green checked shirt sleeves were rolled up above the elbow, but there was no sign of excessive perspiration. Before Danny's arrival, he had hoped to give the master the impression that he was working in the smithy on a favoured horse, but in fact Hickmann was wise to his little affectation.

'Okay, boys, leave him to me.'

Cardine beckoned for Danny to dismount. He did so, and as he was brusquely ordered to remove his gun belt, he did so, but draped it over his arm instead of surrendering it to the *segundo*. Cardine gestured for the hands to take away the dun and tether it. In order to annoy him they elected to take it to a stable and give it a rub down, as an alternative to hay slinging.

Closely following his guide, Danny mounted to the gallery and waited. He was there long enough to take a quick backward glance. This far, there was no sign of the posse coming along. Cardine went in, talked and came out again. He stepped aside for Danny to enter. Again, the young Irishman ignored Cardine and, instead, hung up his gun belt on a hat stand in the narrow hallway, along with his stetson.

Stepping into the big room, he hunched his shoulders a bit, and inclined his head in Hickmann's direction. The name 'Hickmann' burned into timber above the fireplace gave a clue as to the meaning of Circle H.

'You must be Mr Hickmann. I'm sorry to intrude on you. Fact is, I came this way out of necessity.'

Danny looked around, and the owner was curious enough to hear more, so he nodded towards an upright chair, which the newcomer squatted on. Cardine closed the hall door, and seated himself near to it, busying his hands by rolling down his sleeves and replacing his bandanna in the proper place.

'You were sayin', friend?' Hickmann prompted.

'I was sayin' I came this way by necessity. You see, I was takin' my ease up on that big hogsback ridge to the south when a big bunch of riders came up the trail from town. I got to peerin' down at them through curiosity, an' doggone me if they didn't start shootin' up at me, as if I'd committed some crime or somethin' back in town!'

'What's your line of business, amigo?'

Cardine asked, his tone still sounding hostile.

Danny paused in his explanation. He stared at the *segundo* but made no attempt to answer him.

Hickmann lifted his hat, scratched his balding forehead and covered it up again. He shrugged his shoulders. 'I reckon you must be still ahead of the posse right now. You did say it was a posse, didn't you?'

'Not in so many words, Mr Hickmann, but that was what I took them to be. I stayed ahead by gettin' down off the ridge at some speed, takin' risks, you'll allow. An' to keep ahead of them, I crossed some old minin' depot an' kept on comin'. Didn't know anythin' about your outfit till the buildings came in sight.'

Noah Hickmann walked up and down a couple of times, then nodded. He lowered his bulk into a big wooden chair rendered more comfortable by a brown and white cowhide which was draped over it.

'Vic, go tell the womenfolk to bring some coffee, why don't you? An' see how the boys are doin', tallyin' the home herd.'

Cardine took his dismissal well, nodding slightly as he headed for the kitchen. There was a brief exchange of voices before the thump of the *segundo's* boots suggested that he had left the building.

'Tell me one thing, mister,' Hickmann invited. 'If this posse was not really chasin' you, who were they chasin'? Did you happen to see any other riders anywhere around?'

Danny felt himself under close scrutiny from his host. He hesitated about how to word his reply. 'Well, no, not exactly, but I did get to hear some other riders somewhere around the ridge, before the posse got there. I didn't figure where they went to, though. They probably knew the district better than me.'

Hickmann's face was a mask of thoughtfulness over the reply. He hardly noticed when the women knocked on the door, and the Mexican housekeeper pushed in a trolley with cups, saucers and coffee utensils piled on it. Almost at once, the housekeeper went out again, leaving Mrs. Hickmann to pour out the coffee and smile a silent welcome.

Aware that there was a slight atmosphere in the room, Danny rose to his feet and was about to cross over to the table and collect his cup when the door opened again and the brown-haired girl glimpsed earlier came in. She acted as if she had not known about the visitor, but when she allowed her eyes to rest upon him, a remarkable change came over her.

Her animated kite-shaped face lit up with an intense excitement. Her wide-set green eyes flashed. She tossed her long brown wavy hair, which hung around her sloping shoulders like a shapely bell, and tripped across the floor in a short grey riding skirt and dark moccasins.

Danny left his coffee cup on the table and stepped back half a pace, as the attractive girl came straight for him. This was a day of surprises. He had long since decided that the day's doings would somehow set the outline for his life in the future, but this beautiful apparition cut right across the pattern of his thoughts.

He raised his arms sideways, not quite knowing how to react, but all the initiative lay with the girl. She cannoned lightly into him, reached up to his neck and threw her arms around him. On account of the difference in their heights, the passionate kiss she aimed at his cheek landed on the side of his neck.

To keep his balance, he had to put his arms about her and shift his footing. Breathless with surprise, he said nothing.

The kiss ended and the animated face looked up into his own startled countenance. She cried: 'Wilbur! Oh, Wilbur, an' I never thought to see you again, after the accident!'

The rancher's wife had started to her feet, probably to get the girl to disengage herself from the stranger, but Hickmann gestured for her to stay out of it. Danny opened his mouth to politely point out that a mistake had been made, but the eager mouth, hidden behind the bell of hair, was tucked in close to his ear.

She whispered: 'If you've got a posse on your back trail, handsome, you could do yourself an' me, too, a whole lot of good by goin' along with my act. You hear me?'

She backed off, gave him a long hard look, and turned, still holding his hand, to face the older couple.

'Noah, Rachel, this is Wilbur. Wilbur Chase, the man who brought us all the way from Little Creek, Arkansas! Isn't it great he survived the accident, like I did?'

The rancher and his wife accepted the new situation without any great show of enthusiasm. To offset his embarrassment, Danny took the proffered cup of coffee and retired to his chair to drink it. The beverage was hot, but in attempting to drink it he gave himself a short breathing space in which to put the latest development into perspective.

Danny looked startled. So did Rachel and Noah. Only the girl acted as if everything was in order.

'What can you remember of the accident, Wilbur, if it isn't too awful for you to talk about?' the girl persisted.

'Why, er, nothin', miss. Nothin' at all. It's as if it had never happened, as far as I'm concerned!'

Noah started scratching his head, while Rachel rocked back and forth on her chair, her lined sallow face troubled by uncertainty.

'There, there now. I knew it. He got bruised an' knocked about, too. His memory is affected. But I'm sure he'll improve. Now we've met each other again. Keep sayin' my name, eh? Karen. Karen Rillwater. An' think of Little Creek, Arkansas, why don't you?'

She peered hopefully into his face,

and smiled when the embarrassment made him splutter into the hot coffee. As the good beverage trickled down his throat, Danny's outlook changed a little. He was still truly baffled, but he wondered what was in it for him, if he went along with the subtle scheme put forward by this engaging, voluptuous young woman.

She was attractive, all right, and she obviously had connections with the family of Hickmann. But where would it all lead? Did her amorous advances mean that there was something going on between her and the fellow who was supposed to have brought her and someone else all the way from Arkansas? Or was she simply registering emotional relief at being united with a family retainer who had done a responsible escorting job?

Karen Rillwater. Was he going to be hogtied, or had fate shown him the way to make his fortune?

4

The easiest way in which to transmit a message in the days of the moving frontier was probably to fire off a revolver. The sound carried a reasonable distance but it was thought to be a little too distinctive for certain occasions. Cowpunchers of the Circle H had their orders, and on this occasion when a dozen riders headed by the county sheriff made their way across Circle H range, no guns were fired by ranch hands in position for observation. Instead, the hands reverted to a means of communication which someone had read of in a history book. The hunting horn. The day was young still, and owl hoots were out of the question, but the sound emitted by a hunting horn carried for a fair distance and could be relayed again as soon as it had been given by the first 'puncher to observe the posse.

The distant horn had been blown three times when the alarm went around the buildings. This time it was more serious than a single riding stranger, and all the workers on the pay roll had a good idea what to expect.

Noah Hickmann at once put all troublesome speculation out of his mind about the girl, Karen, and her relationship with this stranger who had wandered onto his territory with a rather flimsy excuse for being there.

Hickmann stood up so suddenly that he cracked his head against one of the low beams supporting the ceiling of the main room. Rachel, his wife, gave a suppressed gasp and clutched her throat in a gesture of anxiety.

'Oh dear, hearin' that horn always gives me the shakes. I — I hope it don't mean an accident, or anythin' like that.'

The owner banged out his hat, and restored it to its usual shape, sticking it on his head and glaring at his second wife. 'For cryin' out loud, Rachel, don't you start doin' things to get on my nerves! You know what that signal means. A large bunch of riders. Interlopers! What in tarnation would you have the men do, flap a blanket over a smoky fire? Get a grip on yourself. This could only be a posse drummed up by the sheriff, an' he's bound to come along with his eyes an' ears open, lookin' for information.

'So, I'll be tellin' him what it's necessary for him to know, an' very little more. Is that understood?'

The timid woman nodded and withdrew into herself. She hesitated in front of the girl and the strange young man about withdrawing into the kitchen. Noah, who was at the window, showed a bit more impatience as the tension of the coming visit built up in him.

'Rachel, I don't give a hang whether you stay in the back room or in here, only act natural when the time comes, eh?'

He shrugged his shoulders over her,

and turned his attention to the young couple. 'Now see here, you two. Karen, you're here as a young kinswoman on a visit. That won't seem strange. And I don't care whether this hombre is who you say he is or not. One thing I do care about, though, is what sort of an impression this new sheriff gets of my spread and the Hickmann family.'

Hickmann paused, pacing back and forth between the two of them. Already, Danny was very interested in this special reaction to the hunting horn signal; also, he was interested to know that the rancher had apparently antici-pated a visit from the local sheriff. And that had to mean something.

'Don't bother yourself on my account, Mr Hickmann. I won't do anything to make the peace officers more suspicious,' Danny remarked calmly.

'I'm pleased to hear that, amigo, an' I want you both to be careful how you react to any questions concernin' my brother, Ringo. Leave me to do the explainin' an' don't volunteer any information at all!'

In the low-beamed room it was difficult for the assembled four people to contain their excitement. Karen managed to settle herself in a corner seat, where she stitched coloured thread through a piece of cloth with a heavy needle. Hickmann went out to the bathroom, and was still exuding perspiration when he came back. Danny glanced at him and at once lost his fleeting composure.

Hickmann grudgingly gave him a small cigar to make it seem as if he had been there for some time.

Blinking hard behind plumes of rising smoke, Danny thought about Hickmann's brother, Ringo. Noah had cautioned him about a Ringo. And Ringo was one of the names Danny had heard mentioned when the outlaws were working their way through the secret track ahead of the posse. Ringo and Velasco. Unusual names. If the Ringo on the run was the brother of this well-heeled ranch owner, then he

— Danny — had slipped into very deep waters indeed.

* ★ *

Sheriff Ed Wrangler, sided by his veteran deputy, Mark Landraw, led an arrowhead of thirteen riders jogging across Circle H territory in much the same direction as Danny O'Maldon had done a while earlier.

All the heat seemed to have gone out of the chase, although Wrangler was not altogether disappointed. Being on ranch territory presented a problem of sorts, even to a county peace officer with a fully sworn-in posse. The Circle H had acreage enough to swallow up a small band of riders. It also possessed many head of cattle, and countless small parks where sweating riding-horses could be hidden away from prying eyes.

Wrangler carefully slapped dust out of his dark business suit. He then tidied up his black hard hat and turned his attention to the grey vest which topped his white shirt and tie. Having spent several years in an eastern seaboard police force he was very conscious of his appearance. His full face was clean-shaven and fresh complexioned rather than weather conditioned. Even when his mouth was set in its hardest thin line and the curling blue-black brows were barred across his seemingly unblinking grey eyes, he scarcely looked his thirty-four years.

He patted the rump of his high-stepping roan with a gloved hand, and glanced sideways in the direction of his riding companion.

'So how do you read the pursuit so far, Mark?' he enquired, in a mellow, cultured voice. 'You still think this heist is down to Ringo Hickmann an' that he's somewhere up ahead of us?'

Landraw, a buckskin-wearing westerner who was twenty years older than the sheriff, clicked his tongue and nodded affirmatively.

'Ever since I came this way from New Mexico territory I've known

Ringo Hickmann was a jasper I wanted behind bars,' the deputy remarked, with feeling.

He was a former army scout, who talked noisily through a slightly flattened nose when he was keyed up. He had almost as many lines in his weathered face as the number of trails he had ridden in nearly forty years of saddle travel. The outer ends of his deeply-eroded blue eyes were heavily wrinkled. Short, stiff fair hairs jutted from his nostrils and ears.

'I've seen that hombre a couple of times in towns where heists have been pulled. Them small cruel features stand out in a man's memory, along with his protrudin' eyes an' big ear lobes. He's a renegade, all right, in my book! He's been a road agent in the territory, an' he ain't changed his ways not no-how, he ain't! An' as he's livin' at home, that means his older brother, the spread owner, must be aware what's goin' on, you'll allow.'

'Sure, sure, Mark. Off the record I

agree with you. I believe the hombres in town back there who had the nerve to talk about the robber chief forkin' a familiar palomino boss knew what they were talkin' about, too. But we didn't catch him mounted up, an' his brother is bound to have one or two other yellow hosses tucked away in secret places when we get as far as the buildings.

'If it was Ringo an' his gang, he was stupid to pull a heist so close to home. Sooner or later, we two will pull him in. And that will give us pleasure, don't you agree?'

Landraw rubbed the sides of his boots along his grey gelding's flanks. 'Yer, yer, Ed, I guess we will. I don't figure he'd have robbed the bank in Boot Hill if he'd any notion we were already mounted up an' on the trail lookin' for another criminal. Maybe Ringgo's luck is changin'. Maybe he ain't as lucky as he used to be.'

The deputy lowered his head, so that his features were hidden by the short fringe which hung from the stiff brim of his weathered dun hat. Although he had a reputation for being poker-faced, Landraw liked to get in a few shrewd glances ahead of strangers, before they had a chance to study his own features.

★ ★ ★

Fifteen minutes later, the peace officers and their posse arrived at the spread headquarters and were met promptly and with civility. Wrangler and Landraw were conducted into the house by Noah Hickmann, himself, while the rest of the posse were encouraged to leave their mounts for a spell and take coffee in the bunkhouse.

Fresly washed and wearing a clean shirt, Danny O was planted on an upright chair in a far corner of the room. Dirty coffee cups had been swiftly run out into the kitchen and another lot of gear brought out in their place. The rancher introduced his latest visitors to his wife, the girl Karen,

Danny, who was temporarily answering to the name of Wilbur Chase, and Vic Cardine, who came in on a minor pretext and stayed long enough to shake hands with the lawmen. Noah permitted the visit because he did not want the peace officers to get the idea that the ranch was operating without its full quota of key men. It didn't do to give star toters any unwanted notions.

Noah speeded up his drawl for the visit. He handed out cigars, and insisted that the dusty riders should partake of coffee before any sort of business discussion took place. Karen did the serving. She had changed her blouse for another in grey material, tailored like a man's shirt and piped round the edges with black silk.

Eventually, suspense began to build up in the room. On account of Rachel's nervousness, Noah was compelled to broach the matter of the visit.

'Anythin' special the Circle H can do for you gents? You didn't bring a dozen riders with you just to enjoy the view, I'll allow.'

Wrangler made a pattern by waving his cigar. 'You're right, we were on the prowl. We had two jobs. Somehow, they merged, one into the other. Tell me, were you expectin' riders, Mr Hickmann?'

A few seconds of agonising silence put the Hickmanns on tenterhooks. Karen, sitting on a low padded seat, giggled gracefully. Noah made an effort to be jovial.

'Oh, of course, you're referrin' to our cow horn signals. Well, to be sure, when the boys blow on the horn we expected a group of riders to show up across the range. It don't often happen that way, however. But you could say you were expected, from the time we got the signal. I'd like to ask about the two jobs, if I won't be pryin'.'

Landraw, seated near the front window, took off his fringed hat, nodded easily to the hosts and replaced it.

'An urgent call around breakfast time had us mounted up in Indian Wells. Seems a breed fellow had set fire to his employer's homestead. That is, he burned the house with the folks in it. They managed to get out, somewhat scorched. An' we were able to chase him. If he hadn't been liquored, he would have likely gotten away.'

'Where did you locate him?' Hickmann asked eagerly.

'Greenhorn Gorge,' Sheriff Wrangler put in brightly. 'Not the main gorge, you understand, but that smaller fault which goes off eastward about two miles north of Boot Hill.'

'Did you take him easily?' Danny asked, forgetting that he was supposed to stay silent.

The hard look assembled itself on the sheriff's face.

'No. Not exactly. He went to earth among all those rocks in the lowest part of the fault.'

Wrangler sucked on his cigar, and Landraw took up the story. 'We gave

53

him an ultimatum an' a time limit, an' he didn't react, so we gave him a volley of lead an' that finished him. He's still down there.'

Silence followed this explanation. Hickmann thought the lawmen were in some way issuing a warning. He felt the back of his throat go dry. Having lubricated it again with coffee, he attempted to maintain a low-key conversation.

'No more than he deserved, I guess. But what about the second job? The one that brought you into these parts?'

Landraw asked: 'Mr Hickmann, do you have money in the Red River Cattlemen's Association Bank?'

Hickmann nodded and hurled the butt end of his cigar into the fireplace. 'Why, sure, all Red River County ranchers use the bank. Why do you ask?'

'Because the bank has been robbed of all its ready money. Yours has probably gone, too,' Wrangler explained, matter of factly.

The rancher coloured up, clenched his jaw and gripped the sides of his chair. 'You want to tell me some more about the robbery, gents?'

'Well, it seems some tricky hombres knew the time of day when all the tellers bar one evacuated into the president's room at the back to take coffee. The president an' three of his staff were caught in the back, by visitors to the rear door. They were knocked out with head blows, an' trussed up. Out front, a customer screamed, the one teller reacted an' received a groove in his gun arm for his trouble, an' that was all the resistance amounted to. Five or six men stayed long enough to fill a few canvas money bags, to truss three customers an' then they left. The street was passin' busy, so they fired off their six-guns. An elderly woman who strayed too near to the riders got herself bowled over an' needed a doctor.'

Hickmann was all too clearly aware of the probing eyes of both lawmen resting upon his face. He nodded several times too many and wrestled with his anxiety. Danny's eyes were never still. Karen's seemed overbright, and those of Rachel had a haunted, restless look in them.

'What made you think they came this way, sheriff?' the rancher asked.

Wrangler nodded and replied. 'Havin' dealt with our first criminal we were ridin' into Boot Hill City to take a breather before makin' our way back to the county seat. Only ten minutes separated us at the out-set. Our mounts were not quite as fresh as the outlaws' otherwise we might have rounded them all up long before this.'

'We lost contact somewhere around the hogsback. When we had established they didn't take other directions, Circle H territory seemed to be the only alternative. That reminds me, is your brother, Ringo, anywhere around?'

Landraw had spoken in a normal conversational voice, but the mention of Ringo in his last sentence put a sharper atmosphere in the room.

'Huh?' Noah ejaculated. 'Oh, Ringo. My kid half-brother, you mean! No, he ain't around right now, deputy. Gone off huntin' I wouldn't be surprised. A very restless young hombre, my half-brother. I always thought he ought to have done a spell with the cavalry, but it wasn't to be. What was it reminded you of him?'

The lawmen made him wait for an answer, sharing a private chuckle which had the four listening people all on edge.

Wrangler put up his right hand and snapped his thumb sharply against a finger. 'The palomino, of course. The animal which knocked down the old woman, an' may have killed her. That was a palomino. There aren't many fancy-coloured horses in these parts, you'll allow, Mr Hickmann, you bein' a horse breeder yourself.'

Noah had only time to nod his head, in agreement with the sheriff.

Landraw continued the revelations. 'One or two men in the street, who got a good look at the outlaws as they rode through said the galoot forkin' the palomino had somethin' different about his hat. I don't suppose you could help us on that, Mr Hickmann.'

The rancher spluttered and blustered. He knew full well that his brother had a band of small coins round his hat where other — more modest — men wore a simple leather strap or possibly a bit of snake-skin.

Karen brightly talked about differing colours, while Rachel talked about the way different riders mauled about their hat brims. The tension in the room appeared to subside a little. Wrangler was the one to start a conversation about Karen and the purpose of her stay on the ranch.

The lawmen listened with close attention as she described her parents as being aged. Her Pa was arthritic. Her Ma had become increasingly deaf, and was quite withdrawn at times from everyday affairs. The Rillwaters' real estate business was in the capable hands of a manager named Abraham Trencher.

On account of Karen's being chesty at times, the old folks had decided to send her, along with a companion, Kate-Ellen Armour, on the long journey to the Panhandle. A long-time servant of the family, Wilbur Chase, had been given the responsible job of driving them in the surrey, seeing to their lodgings on the way, and guarding them against all possible dangers on the way to the Hickmanns' ranch.

All had gone well until Wilbur took the Gorge trail, instead of the more frequently used townlinking tracks. The Gorge was a long, meandering rock fault with a scenic track along its winding lowest grade. It snaked back and forth, crossing the regular trails over a distance of some fifteen miles, flirting with three towns but not doing anyone who used it a lot of good.

There had been hazards on the long journey from Little Creek, Arkansas, but nothing so treacherous as the last few miles along Greenhorn Gorge. Something had startled the fine pair of horses. They had panicked, and the surrey had left the route, throwing out its three occupants and all the clothing and finery in the carrying cases.

All three travellers had suffered. Karen had recovered first, and found her way to the ranch. Wilbur had shown up just a short while ago, his memory not yet fully restored. This far, Kate-Ellen Armour was still missing and feared dead.

Danny O came out of a daze as the two peace officers came to their feet and professed themselves ready to move on. Noah asked them to ride freely over his territory, if they had the slightest suspicion that outlaws were hiding out on it, and the posse leaders took him at his word.

Wrangler and Landraw were still on the front gallery when Danny moved across to Karen and asked a question.

'Say, Karen, what sort of a person is your companion? This girl, Kate-Ellen?'

The girl rounded on him silently and kicked his shin with a moccasined foot. 'Hush, man! Do you want to ruin everything?'

Danny thought her reaction was a bit unfair, as she had been the one to establish that his memory had been affected, but he kept quiet until the riders had bunched and ridden off in a tight group.

5

A half-hour after the peace officers had gone off, taking the posse riders with them, Noah Hickmann was in the kitchen of the ranch house, stripped to the waist and leaning over the big all-purpose sink. Rachel, his wife, was slowly tipping water over him, enabling him to freshen up after the ordeal of staying calm in front of his visitors, under pressure.

Five minutes earlier, Karen Rillwater, accompanied by Danny O, still tentatively using the name of Wilbur Chase, had strolled out at the rear of the buildings. They had been given time to discuss their past at length, and without anyone being close enough to overhear.

Shortly after Rachel had handed Noah the towel, there was a knock at the kitchen door. The woman crossed over and opened it. Noah stopped towelling his head to listen.

'It's me, Mrs Hickmann, I wondered if your husband had any odd chores he specially wanted me to do, while Vic is away chaperonin' the visitors.'

The sallow-faced woman backed away, waiting for her husband to answer the query. The rancher's eyebrows climbed his forehead. He blinked in surprise, then chuckled to himself and started to shake his head.

'Checks an' balances is what we have here on the Circle H! Ain't that so, wife? Cardine checks on everybody, without bein' asked, most of the time. An' little Dixie checks on Vic. I wonder what Vic would think if he knew Dixie was spyin' on him?'

Dixie, just outside the door, gasped. 'I didn't mean it that way, Boss. I must have been thinkin' aloud. I guess I'm sorry I troubled you.'

'All right, Dixie, I won't tell him. Stick around, fairly close. I might have somethin' different for you, an' then I might not.'

The diminutive cowpuncher thanked Hickmann profusely, and left. Rachel began to wring her hands, her face working with nerves.

'Tell me, husband, what do you think about Ringo? Is he goin' to be captured by the posse? Is he? Because if he is taken, it could bring big trouble to you. Sooner or later, he's goin' to bring you an' this outfit you worked so hard to build up into disrepute. Even, even if he can't stop himself doin' robberies, I don't think he should have busted into a bank so near home! A bank which had *your* money in it! It doesn't make sense to me, Noah, an' I have to say that. Even if he is your half-brother.'

The rancher made his wife sit down in a rocker. He made her relax, while he did some thinking.

'He sure as hell was a darned fool to pull anythin' as near home as Boot Hill City. Already we have hombres conjecturin' about that big palomino hoss he forks. I'm goin' to have to do somethin' about Ringo one of these days, even if

64

the law doesn't catch up with him. Trouble is, I don't know what to do for the best.'

Noah sank into a chair, the towel slung between his hands, and his rounded chin resting in it. Rachel stopped the rocking chair.

'An' that young man turnin' up like he did. If her Pa didn't have all that money, back in Little Creek, Arkansas, I'd be inclined to think she was on the make. Tryin' to extract money or privileges out of us Hickmanns.'

Noah sniffed hard, and wagged a horny finger at her. 'You're shrewd, Rachel. I admire you for it. Somethin's got to give, in the matter of our heiress, Miss Karen Rillwater. When she came all the way here, with my permission, she was supposed to bring a consider-able amount of money or valuables with her.

'In the event she fancied marryin' Ringo, he was to get most of the profit. If there was no marriage rigged up, an' she wanted to stay, some of that dowry or whatever you call it was supposed to come my way for allowin' her to take up permanent residence with us.

'That accident, in the gorge, has kind of mixed things up. Ringo ain't particularly interested in the girl, although I'll allow she's mighty pretty, an' strong enough to raise a decent family. So, if my charmin' half-brother would rather rob others than receive what could rightly be his, I say what about me? Where's this treasure box the girl mumbles about? I don't even know if we're ever goin' to find it!'

'Is that young man genuine?' Rachel asked, frowning.

Noah shrugged into a clean shirt, his mouth set in a tight line and his head shaking sagely from side to side.

'I don't rightly know. He panicked a bit, to do with the posse. But then most hombres get the jitters when a load of mean lawmen come seekin' a target. We'll have to see. Maybe he's just driftin', livin' on his wits, or there's a chance he's who she says he is, an' his

66

mind has suffered. Even if he ain't who she says he is, it's just possible he might try to help her. An' if he assists her by findin' what I'm interested in, I'll be real pleased.'

Rachel started to chuckle to herself. The talk and the rocking gradually restored her to something like her normal composure.

★   ★   ★

On the way out, through the buildings, Karen slipped her arm through Danny's and whispered for him to mime his talk, so as not to give anything away to anyone who might be listening.

Danny, who did not know the layout of the spread, spent a good deal of time examining what he could see of the buildings, and the horses in the extensive pole corral. Presently, Karen cleared her throat and coughed; a gentle, confidential sound which drew back her escort's attention. She minced along daintily in her moccasins, still dressed in her grey blouse and short skirt, but with her long brown hair tied at the nape of her neck in a white ribbon. On her head she had a big straw hat, shaped like a Texan's stetson, but with a white silk ribbon serving as a band.

She shifted her hand, gently gripping Danny's, and looking up into his face, she whispered: 'I'm sorry I threw myself at you like I did, mister. But, well, I was in a bit of a spot an' I thought I saw a chance to get myself out of it. If you like, you can tell me your real name now.'

She flashed him a smile which revealed fine teeth and a certain captivating promise. Danny admired her openly, and started to react, but before telling her his real name, he happened to look back and the sight of the tall, gangling bow-legged figure of Vic Cardine, obviously following them, made him groan and seal his lips.

Karen clicked her tongue. 'He's goin' to follow us to make sure we don't get up to any mischief. But don't you worry too much about Vic Cardine. Old Noah Hickmann doesn't like him as much as you might think. Noah's half-brother, Ringo, is the likely one to be taken into partnership, or to take over, if anything happened to Noah.

'Vic is kin, all right, but he's just, well, sort of sniffin' around. He stays well in the background when Ringo is around. You'll see how it is, if an' when younger brother shows up.'

Danny shrugged in an exaggerated fashion. He lengthened his stride, and Karen kept pace with him. Cardine noted the increase in pace, but he simply smirked and adjusted the cradling of his rifle in the crook of his right arm.

'I don't figure you're doin' yourself any good, Karen, expectin' me to stick around here,' Danny remarked bluntly. 'I don't go for entanglements. I spoke the truth when I said I had arrived on Hickmann property by mistake. Me, I drift! Lots of men do, just the way I do.

I look out for opportunities, an' when the goin' gets a bit rough or problems crop up, I fork my bronc an' hightail it for other parts. Places where there's room to breathe. No entanglements, you hear?'

Karen flexed and unflexed the fingers of the hand which was in his. She lowered her head, so that he could not see her face. They walked on, negotiated a small hill and went on down the other side. A few hundred yards ahead sunlight sparkled on a flowing creek, partially hidden by patches of fern, bushes and two or three large willow trees.

Presently, Danny felt so curious about her that he halted their advance, and tilted her head up by lifting her chin. The big green eyes were wet with tears. Two tiny trickles had started down her cheeks. The full, mobile mouth trembled uncertainly.

'Hey, hey, there's no need for tears, I'll warrant.' He pulled her closer and leaned down and kissed her with great tenderness, surprising himself with his own sensitivity. 'Untie my bandanna, an' dab your cheeks with it. I reckon we might as well give that interferin' Cardine fellow something to see for his trouble.'

Totally ignoring the unwanted escort, who had slowed down to keep his distance, Karen did as Danny had suggested, replacing the bandanna and holding it in place about his neck while he kissed her with greater feeling.

Cardine's voice was slightly off-key as he mocked them with derisory laughter. Danny started to stiffen up when he heard it, but Karen took no notice.

'You won't make so free with that female when Ringo gets back!'

Their lips came apart. Danny could almost read her thoughts. He felt that inwardly she was begging him to spirit her away before life became any more complicated by the return of the unpredictable, elusive Hickmann.

'I don't rightly know what you hoped to achieve, bringin' me down to the creek like this, Karen, but I sure as hell would like to take a rise out of that hombre back there, Cardine. How would it be if we worked out a plan to give him the slip? You want to be in on somethin' like that?'

Karen giggled and feverishly kissed him again. Then she backed off and resumed the stroll towards the water. Soon, they came to a kind of hollow in the nearside bank. Side by side, they studied the rippling waters as they sped past.

'I wonder what goes on on the other side?' Karen murmured wistfully. 'I have this yearnin' to see what the terrain is like around that bend over there. What do you think? Is there any chance we can get across? Wouldn't it be great if we could get over there, secretly, an' leave the Cardine hombre back here?'

Karen stopped dabbing away at the shallows with her moccasined foot. Danny's prolonged silence had at last affected her. He was looking away to his right, staring under the overhanging branches of huge willow tree at water level.

'The water's deep enough to have to swim, or take a boat,' Danny murmured. 'I wonder if our escort knows about that punt?'

'That *what*?'

'The punt, hidden there under the branch. A long, shallow, flat-bottomed boat, propelled by a long pole which is supposed to touch the bottom when it is used. Squared off at each end. There could be a paddle, I suppose. Let's look into it.'

He grasped her by the hand, ducked into a crouch and brushed his way under the dipping foliage. Somewhere above the hollow, Cardine clicked the mechanism of his rifle. The couple kept quite still, like children playing a hiding game. The gun lever clicked a second time; this revealed that Cardine had moved up stream.

'He's lost us, for the moment,' Danny whispered. 'Come on. Get in. There's no pole, but I can see a paddle. I think it's watertight.'

Karen gasped, not having considered if the light craft was waterworthy. She glanced up into her companion's face and had her confidence restored. Already, she was beginning to rely upon him, even though he seemed quite against doing anything to help her permanently.

Danny stood with one booted foot on either side of the boat, holding up the long springy branch with his back. Karen moved along to the bow, doubled up small and actually passing through the arch of his legs. They exchanged information by mime, and after nodding two or three times Karen squared off her straw hat and worked the paddle from a kneeling position, well forward. For a minute or two, Danny had to fend off encroaching branches, and then they were clear. The current turned the bow end slowly downstream, so that Karen had to do all her work over one side.

Danny sprawled out, near the stern. He rolled up a sleeve and used his arm over the side to help her.

'Hey, you know a lot about small boats for a horse-ridin' drifter, amigo. How come?'

Her partner chuckled. 'My real father was Captain Abraham O'Maldon. When he was ashore in Frisco, he used to like to take my mother an' me out in small boats. It kind of relaxed him.'

'What did you say your real first name was?'

'Danny. Danny O, the substitute parents used to call me, back in the days when my Ma and Pa had been drowned in a shipwreck. The others put me through a good school with Pa's money. Then I got foot loose. Got into trouble with the police. One time I did something I was ashamed of. Something *they* wouldn't want to know about. So I strung a few things together and crossed the Rockies with a wagon train. Been on this side ever since. So where is Vic Cardine? We're half across an' he ain't shown up yet.'

Karen stopped paddling. As the punt reacted, a hoarse cry came from the bank they had left, well upstream. Cardine cursed them heartily, brought up his rifle and drew a make-believe sighting on them. Kneeling in an upright position, half way up the boat, Danny pulled off his hat and waved it.

Cardine fidgeted about for a time, and then he seemed to come to a decision. He fired a single shot fairly high between the two punters who reacted smartly. Danny went forward, and from then on the two of them plied their craft almost lying prone from near the bow.

When they ran it ashore, Cardine had disappeared from view. His withdrawal bothered Danny for a minute or two, but Karen took up the leadership as they scrambled clear and he went willingly along with her, not pausing until they had moved about thirty yards from the creek and were crouched low in a warm bed of screening fern.

Of their observer there was no sign. Gradually, they relaxed. The bullet had obviously been fired in a mood of frustration. Karen removed her hat, pulled out her hair ribbon and went to work on her hair with a wide comb. Danny stretched out on his back, tilted his stetson over his eyes and watched her.

Presently, she chuckled, and glanced back at him.

'So we shook him off,' the young drifter murmured. 'Big deal.'

He closed his eyes for a minute or more, and when he opened them his hat was removed and the same comb was being gently pulled through his own fine, short brown hair.

'You have auburn highlights in your hair, Danny.'

He was about to agree, but Karen bent low over him and kissed him. It was an entirely pleasant sensation, but Danny had little experience with cuddlesome girls. His heart began to thump with the excitement. He liked the way her long tresses tickled his face, but he had a feeling he was in some sort of a tender trap. He opened his blue eyes, which usually appeared to be so innocent, and became aware of Karen's green ones quite close to his own.

She murmured: 'What's the matter, Danny? Don't you find me attractive? Shucks, I'm in a fix. I need help. You happen along, an' you're a real nice fellow with no ties. I don't make a practice of throwin' myself at young men, I can assure you!'

She was getting angry, which made her attractive in another sort of way. He tried to distract her.

'What's it like, bein' an heiress, a young woman who will inherit?'

The clear green eyes swam with tears again. 'I don't know, Danny. Because you see I'm not what I make out to be.' Her voice rose in volume, very slightly. 'I'm not Karen Rillwater, at all. I'm only her girl companion, Kate-Ellen Armour. My folks died in an epidemic, you see, an' the Rillwaters were good to me because their daughter needed a companion an' helpmate of her own age.

'I made out I was Karen, after the accident. I don't even know if she's alive or not! I don't think she is, though, because otherwise she'd have turned up at the Circle H an' denounced me before now. I'm an impostor, you see. Not quite what people think me.

'But I don't make a habit of cheatin'! This far in my life, I've been strictly honest, an' now I'm in over my head. I don't want to marry that beast, Ringo, like the real Karen was supposed to do, an' I can't come up with the treasure-box which we were supposed to be bringin' along to hand over to Karen's intended, or to Noah, if he allowed her to stay permanently.'

Tears gradually engulfed her, and for the second time her distress brought out a warm, gentle side of Danny's nature; a side of him which he did not know much about. He stroked her hair and made soothing noises.

He said: 'Take it easy, little one. I guess we orphans have got to stick together, eh?'

There was so much hope, so much optimism reflected in her eyes that Danny winced, wondering if he had made her expect too much. Even now, his most compelling urge to cut and run, had the upper hand. But he could not say anything to undermine her fragile confidence.

Slowly, he eased her to her feet, gently brushed her down and looked her over. He wondered what he could do to help her without becoming fully involved in her undoubtedly complicated, problematical life.

Hand in hand, they strolled back to the bank and the punt. 'Maybe I can help you to locate that missin' box you spoke of, before I move on again. What do you think?'

She nodded several times, hazarded a glance or two up at his face and gradually recovered herself. 'Okay,

Danny, maybe you could. Only don't do it out of charity, will you? You bein' a really nice guy. Much better lookin' an' surely more desirable than the real Wilbur Chase. Although he had his points, I guess.'

The girl became thoughtful as they took their places in the punt once more. Danny did not intrude upon her privacy. There was a bond, of sorts, between them. Each found the other's company congenial, and did not want this short, private excursion into Circle H territory to come to an end.

Consequently, they did not pull as strongly as they might have done, in making the return crossing. Neither of them showed any concern when the current carried them around the bend of the creek. Even when they saw the low wooden footbridge linking one bank to the other, it was not an occasion for surprise.

Vic Cardine only came back into their thoughts when his boots began to have a flat-footed effect upon the timbers of the bridge, and they gradually became aware of the fact that he also had crossed over; that he was on his way back, as they were.

His homely features writhed with the effect of his triumphant smirk. He tapped gently on the boards with the butt of his rifle and strove to find words which would shatter them. He did not have to try very hard.

'Glad you didn't stay over there too long, folks, I'll be glad to get back to the boss, 'cause I want to tell him you are both impostors! You're no better than a drifter an' a travellin' lady's paid companion! I wonder how little brother, Ringo, will react to that, eh?'

After a brief pause, during which anger drove the punt across the current, Danny thought up words sufficiently disquieting to tame the eavesdropper.

'How would it be if we, the two of us, told lies about you to that hair-trigger tempered cousin of yours? I'm sure we could cook up a neat little tale to make Ringo drive you off the Circle H for good!'

Even as he made the threat, Danny knew it was scarcely possible that the Hickmanns would believe a story brought to them by an unknown passing-through drifter. However, Cardine did become thoughtful, and he gave them no cause for complaint on the way back to the ranch buildings.

6

The continuing lack of news about Ringo Hickmann meant that the tense atmosphere over the home buildings of the spread persisted. And yet those who could went about their daily tasks and tried to give one another the impression that all was normal.

While the trio were coming back from the creek, most of the cowpunchers were engaged in a horseshoe tossing contest at the back of the bunkhouse. Gradually, men were eliminated. The three ahead of the field were the stoop-shouldered blacksmith, his negro striker and a man named Latigo who was always practising throws with long and short lariats.

Dixie went over and patted the back of Ah Wong, the chef, who had kept up with the leaders through several rounds. The small man had a huge appetite, and consequently he stayed on the right side of the cook wherever possible.

As Latigo's arms tired, so his throwing became erratic. After a last despairing throw which fell beyond the pin and bounced further away, Latigo raised his arms and admitted himself beaten. That left the ageing blacksmith and his muscular, greying striker to end the contest between the two of them.

Harshly blending voices rose and fell as the shoes were tossed and the fortunes of the last pair fluctuated. Noah Hickmann always made a point of watching the finishing shots in such contests. He was good at it himself, and he thought his presence kept him in touch with his boys at an informal level. That being so, he stopped the old weathered rocker on the front gallery of the house, tried to push out of his mind his forebodings about Ringo, and strolled over to join the crowd of shouting hands.

Danny and Kate-Ellen, who also had problems, avoided the bunkhouse area and skirted the house, wondering what sort of a mood Noah would be in when they renewed contact. The girl looked into all the windows and decided that Noah wasn't there. She guessed where he was. Cardine was no longer behind them, and Kate-Ellen allowed a brief shudder of panic to transmit itself from her to Danny. She was shaking when he drew her away from the house and into the smithy, which was still quite warm from a recent session of work.

'Talk to me about the town you came from, an' give me a few details I can pretend to remember,' Danny urged, to try and allay her fears.

The girl responded, and she was still talking excitedly when they left the smithy and went to the nearest stable, where a few of the best riding horses were sprawling about at their ease. Through the stable window, they saw Cardine move in behind the crowd at the shoe-tossing contest.

'He just can't wait to turn Noah against us,' Kate-Ellen murmured. 'I figure fate is not on our side, Danny. The next thing, I'll be callin' you Danny in front of the others, instead of Wilbur.'

'What do your folks, your friends call you when you're in company?' Danny asked, unexpectedly.

'Oh, just Katie, I guess,' the girl responded. 'I'd like to hear my real name come off your lips, but don't make the mistake of sayin' it in public, will you? Shucks, we sure are up against it, aren't we?'

Danny embraced her, tidied up her face with his bandanna and went on with the inspection of the riding horses.

$$\star \quad \star \quad \star$$

A great roar of enthusiasm filled the air as Noah Hickmann out-threw the smith and the striker. Noah danced up and down the throwing area with his arms above his head. He hurled his hat in the air and almost lost his balance as he manoeuvred his way under it again.

By this time, Ah Wong had withdrawn from the playing area. A single clang on a metal triangle warned the hired hands that the evening meal was about ready. Many of the men were always hungry and they started to amble away without further ado. Cardine pushed his way through some of those who remained and headed straight for the master, who began to restrain himself as they came together.

'Nice goin', Boss! I ain't never seen you throw better, an' I've got news for you!'

Noah paused with his fists on his hips, breathing hard and his face working. 'Glad you got back all right, Vic! Tell me, where are Karen an' that Wilbur fellow?'

This question took the *segundo* by surprise. He had not anticipated it. His jaw dropped a little as he suppressed his startling news and thought about an answer.

'Why, some place around, Boss. They came back just ahead of me, from the creek. In the house, I suppose. It ain't likely they lit out for other parts, is it?'

The rest of the hands had gone into the bunkhouse by this time, and Noah walked away from the throwing pit, striding towards the back of the house. As he walked, he dabbed his neck and forehead with a bandanna.

Cardine's conjectural answer annoyed him. 'Why, surely you'd be the one to answer that question, Vic, seein' as how you've appointed yourself as unofficial guard to the two of them.'

Hickmann outstepped Cardine as the *segundo* strove to regain his composure. 'Boss, I crossed over the creek an' got near enough to hear what they was talkin' about! That there girl, Karen, ain't Karen at all! She's the hired female companion, no less! An' the hombre who she said was Wilbur Chase answers to the name of Danny! Now, what do you say to that?'

Cardine danced round the front of the rancher and forced him to stop. Hickmann did so, and while he was pondering what he had just been told, a voice came from the nearest stable.

'Don't you believe a word of it, Noah!' the girl called. 'He's lyin', tryin' to ingratiate himself with you, for personal gain!'

The two men turned round sharply to face the stable, but even so Kate-Ellen's flying figure took them by surprise. She hurled herself across the intervening space and took a swing at Cardine, putting a red patch down the side of his face.

He stepped back a pace, one hand clutching the side of his head. He muttered: 'Surely, Noah, you ain't goin' to believe her instead of me?'

Katie was beating his chest and another wild swing caught him on the ear. Cardine staggered back again. He threw her off, and as she came in once more with both fists whirling, he swung back at her. The back of his hand caught her hard across the side of the head, and knocked her backwards. She fell to the ground, shaken and slightly dazed. Just when all three were wondering about him, Danny emerged from the stable and bent down beside Katie.

'I don't know what it is about this Cardine fellow, Mr. Hickmann, but he sure has the makings of a brawler, lashin' away like that at a defenceless young woman. Can't you do anythin' about him?'

Danny turned and glanced up quizzically at the rancher. Hickmann hesitated. Perhaps he thought a few healthy exchanges might go a long way to improve failing memories. As soon as he saw that the rancher was uncertain of himself, Cardine crouched and advanced on Danny, intending to knock him out with a single blow.

In order to protect Katie, who was recovering slowly, the young drifter rose swiftly and took a step towards the *segundo*. Taken unawares, Cardine received a braced elbow not far above his waistline. He gagged as the air went out of him, and had to back off and rest his hands against the wall of the stable.

During the brief respite, Danny helped Katie to her feet and assisted her across the open ground to the rear gallery of the house. There, she slumped into a sitting position where she could recover slowly. Hickmann casually joined her without showing pleasure or displeasure over the recent exchanges. No one else appeared. Hickmann glanced at the young woman and noticed her toying with a gold ring on her third finger. He recollected that she had always worn it since she turned up unexpectedly a few weeks earlier. Furthermore, the initials on the ring were quite plain to see. 'K.R.'

Cardine straightened up cautiously, and approached Danny, who was angry and willing to fight, although he did not claim to have any special skill with his fists. Danny discarded his hat, and made ready.

'Who fired that rifle shot?' Hickmann enquired, distracting both men.

'I did!' Cardine put in smartly.

Before he could go on, Danny interrupted. 'He wasn't stalkin' an unarmed man an' a girl with a loaded rifle! If you ask me, he was shootin' at game birds!'

Bristling with anger, Cardine straightened up and paused. Danny rushed in and struck him a glancing blow on the right side of his head which cancelled out Cardine's wordy protest. The round-shouldered foreman lost his hat and came forward with both arms flailing.

Several punches missed because he wasn't looking at his target, but eventually a swinging hook caught Danny on the ear and sent him reeling back in the direction of the stable. Cardine lowered his head and charged. A kick was deflected to the shoulder. Unable to rise, Danny adroitly moved backwards, on his knees, and when he rose Vic's bony forehead connected with his nose and brought tears of pain to the brown-haired young man's eyes.

A punch landed high in Danny's chest, bearing him back to the wall.

Cardine blundered in, moving fast, swung a clubbing jab at the head, and missed — hitting the wall. Danny then scored quickly three times with short-arm blows to the chest. Cardine sagged against him, and a crooked blow aimed at his neck took a lot of steam out of him.

After that, Danny literally hit him away from the wall. The *segundo* was by no means out on his feet, but he had lost the vital energy needed to make the running. So Danny advanced. Two punches out of three were on target. Perhaps one of each of those two did some damage. For a non-pugilistic character he was doing quite well.

A punch between the eyes sent Cardine down on his knees. He stayed that way, upright from the knees and would no doubt have been knocked unconscious. Two things saved him. A last, noisy clanging on the triangle for missing diners, and a sudden show of impatience on the part of Hickmann.

'All right, boys, break it up! The two

of you brightened up an otherwise borin' evenin'. Vic, go get yourself under the pump. Clean up a little, an' don't answer too many questions when you go for your meal.'

'An' you, Karen, if that's truly your name. Take the other fellow into the kitchen. Get Fermina to swab him down a bit, or do it yourself if she's busy. Tell the house Chase will be dinin' with us an' that I've got a healthy appetite. *Comprende?*'

Hickmann stomped off in the direction of the smithy. Cardine came erect with an effort. He meandered towards his hat, collected it and went off to the outside pump without looking back. Danny walked slowly over to the steps and slumped into a sitting position beside Katie. His head sagged against her.

'My, my old Pa always used to say women were trouble. Before you know where you are, they have you fightin' over 'em, actin' like you are ten feet tall, an' it's true! I've just proved it!'

Katie kissed him, on the lips. He winced over a small cut in his upper one, and said 'Ouch.' Aiming to assist her, he moved his hands clumsily to her face, gently cradling it, one hand on each side. This time Katie gasped. One of her cheeks was sore on account of Cardine hitting her.

Danny remarked: 'I'll kill him!'

He made a determined effort to rise to his feet, but two factors dissuaded him. His legs were feeling acutely tired, and Katie's arms were restraining him. So he gave up trying and submitted to having his mouth and cheeks kissed all over again.

Presently, he groaned. 'Oh, Katie, what the hell.'

'Not Katie, Danny. Karen. Remember?'

'Well, Karen, then. I believe I told you I wasn't up to much. I don't shoot well. I'm not much of a fighter, am I?'

From two inches apart the clear green eyes challenged the blue ones. 'I thought you did really well back there, Wilbur. He's a mite taller than you are, an' his arms are longer. But you got the better of him, didn't you? I had the feelin' you even surprised yourself!'

Behind them, the kitchen outer door opened an inch or two, and then it swung back all the way. Rachel Hickmann and Fermina, the house-keeper, peered out side by side.

'Hm, seems to me as if this here young feller won the fight. What do you say, Fermina?'

'Si, señora. If we take him indoors an' patch him up a little he'll grace the table for supper!'

Suddenly, Katie had made a full recovery. The old women exchanged covert eyeglances as the girl led Danny to the big wash bowl, already full of soapy water and began to minister to him. Her glances were so fierce that the other women retired to the dining room. Danny was still an unknown quantity to them but Vic Cardine was heartily disliked by both.

The kitchen was full of gusty whispers. 'If the talk gets round to the

97

scene of the accident, for goodness'
sake talk about that — that Greenhorn
Gorge, Kay — Karen, 'cause it's a
complete mystery to me. You hear?'

The master's footsteps out of doors
put an end to their conversation.

7

The beef and the fruit pie went down well. Noah Hickmann liked his food and he was usually in a mellow mood by the time the evening meal had gone down and the coffee pot had been emptied. Out on the front gallery, with the shadows beginning to draw in a little, the rancher took his two guests. For himself, he lighted one of his big cigars, the ones he reserved for that time of the evening. An offer of one was made to Danny, who thought Hickmann must have some confidence in him. However, Danny declined the good cigar and asked for a smaller one. He was gambling in a way. Noah might very well be offended if one of his best smokes was refused by an uninvited guest. On the other hand, if he was really miserly with them, he could just as easily take the refusal as a kindly act.

The sighs of satisfaction as the creaking rocking chair went into action led Danny to believe that he had done the right thing.

'Let's not talk any more about trust,' Noah remarked, as smoke zigzagged from his cigar. 'Let's say I approve of your offer, Wilbur, to go lookin' for that missin' box in the gorge. Along with Karen, here, an' anyone else I choose to send along with you. How will that be?'

Danny shrugged and nodded several times. 'The box in question is not my property. I'm makin' the offer to help Karen. An' indirectly, perhaps, yourself. I just hope no two-bit ordinary drifter hasn't found it already an' gone off to places unknown.'

'An' so say all of us,' Katie put in fervently.

The conversation then drifted to other things of less moment. The weather, the rearing of cows and the training of horses. Perhaps an hour after the sun had dipped in the west, Noah yawned hugely and muttered to himself.

'Now see here, young fellow, I hope you won't take it amiss, but I'm goin' to ask you to spread your roll in the windmill tonight. It's clean fresh on the top floor an' you'll have nothin' to bother about till Ah Wong starts rousin' the troops tomorrow mornin'. Now, what do you say? Will you play things my way?'

Danny chuckled. 'I can't rightly expect to occupy a room in the house, an' I wouldn't know anyone in the bunkhouse, so I guess the mill is as good a place as any for a man like me, who turned up unexpected.'

Hickmann came to his feet smartly. Danny and Karen hestitated, and eventually Danny gave her a brief hug and peck on the cheek.

The rancher whistled. As a result, Dixie, the undersized cowhand came strolling over from the smithy with his hands in his pockets.

'Somethin' you want, Boss?'

'Yer, Wilbur, here, is sleepin' in the mill tonight. Show him up to the top floor, an' advise him about the lamp an' such. I reckon he's ready to sleep, right now.'

Having called his 'goodnight' to all and sundry, the rancher stepped indoors and called Karen in after him. Dixie escorted Danny to the stable, where his bedroll was located and then up into the mill, with its familiar cereal smell. Soon, they had the roll spread out and the lamp swinging from a bracket, not too close to the tinder-dry corn. Dixie teased him about mice, Danny responded, and then the former left, negotiating the narrow, worn wooden stairs without difficulty, due to familiarity.

Danny opened the double shutters and peered out. He was just in time to see Dixie emerge at the bottom swinging a big key on a ring. Suspicions poured back into the visitor's mind.

'Hey, Dixie, you haven't locked the door, surely?'

'Sure, Wilbur. The boss always locks in guests who stay in the mill. It's a habit, I guess. You can give him a shout if you want, but any sort of disturbance just when he's retirin' puts him in a bad mood.'

Danny thought hurriedly about yelling a message to the big house, but having regard for all the cowpunchers and the regular users of the house, he finally decided against causing an uproar. But he was far from pleased with his latest discovery. If Hickmann made a habit of putting casual visitors in the mill, perhaps he had secret plans for their future. Perhaps Noah was as much of a schemer as his devious half-brother. Maybe his only interest was in the dowry, which Karen was supposed to have brought with her.

If gain was his only aim, then the possible fate of Katie and himself did not bear thinking about.

Several of the buildings were clearly visible from Danny's eyrie. He felt that he was being observed, and yet he

103

could not detect any observers. There were lights in the house, the bunk-house, the galley and the smithy, apart from the mill.

Minus his boots, the prisoner in the mill began to ponder the possibility of leaving the mill and the spread before morning. He paced about, occasionally knocking his head on the surrounding woodwork. The source of the machinery interested him. He unhooked the available lamp and examined it more closely.

The brake lever was in position, otherwise the creaking of the various moving parts would have denied him sleep. Purely out of curiosity, he took the brake off and stood back, while the sails moved under the influence of the feeble breeze. Through his aperture, he was able to see them making their circle in the air.

Danny had not seen Dixie's earlier spectacular descent, by way of the sail. Moreover, such a descent was likely to be noticed, and that would gainsay any advantage gained by escaping from the building. So, after a brief survey of the working parts, he switched off again, and thought about escape.

On his own, he felt he could do it. Given time, he could break through a locked door. Or he could make a descent by rope, if the coil of rope stowed in a corner of the upper chamber happened to be long enough. One way or another, he was going to get out. If it had not been for the key incident, he would have chanced his arm with Katie on the Circle H for a day or two longer: carried out his promise to explore the gorge for the missing article, too. But not now.

So, Katie was the problem. What were her priorities? he wondered. If she put freedom first, then she would not hesitate to make a break with him in the middle of the night. If she wanted to recover the box more than anything else, there was still a chance that he could go off with her — the two of them alone — and make the search . . .

In the event of his getting out of the mill undetected, she could possibly be located and asked. If she disapproved of his escape by darkness, then he could go alone: but the very prospect of leaving without her brought a deep scowl to his face. She had thrown herself upon him with all her problems, and now — when he could slip away — he did not want to go without her.

He smoked a small cigar, sitting with his legs crossed near the shuttered aperture, rocking himself backwards and forwards. Locating his horse and saddle was no problem. He had already been in the stable where the dun gelding was kept. And he had seen the piebald riding horse which had been put at the girl's disposal.

A huge yawn warned him that sleep was not far off. He rubbed out the butt of his cigar with great care, came to his feet and hauled the rope out of the corner. It was rather thick for easy manipulation, but he fixed one end round a supporting wooden bracket and lowered the loose end out of the aperture. Foot by foot it went, lower and lower. When he had only about six feet left in hand, he wished he had tied a weight of some sort to the lower end.

To a man leaning out, and looking straight down in a prone position the earth looked a goodly distance below. Shrugging off the mildest touch of vertigo, he slung his boots round his neck, blew out the lamp and wriggled over the narrow sill.

Gripping the rope was painful to his feet, but he felt sure that he could not have achieved a grip at all with his riding boots which were shiny surfaced and too stiff. Faint sounds drifted up to him, made his neck hairs bristle. It was fortunate that Noah Hickmann did not believe in having dogs around the spread, otherwise this little venture would have been doomed at the outset.

As he swung, his arms taking most of the pressure, the buildings slowly cavorted from one side to the other; the house, the house riding stable, the smithy, the huge barn. The dark wooden sides of the windmill next, and then painted corral posts and rails, followed by more stables, the galley and the bunkhouse.

A faint light showed in the galley and the bunkhouse, and a slight glow in the smithy, but nothing happened to show imminent activity. His feet gained a bit of relief as the last of the rope was reached. He would have rested, but his aching arms and shoulders had taken a lot of punishment, and some muscles were starting to jump, so he continued the arm work and only hesitated very briefly to look down, before he let go.

Less than six feet between the end of the rope and the soft ground, and yet it was difficult to gauge exactly the drop, and so some strain in his lower muscles occurred. Having landed, he bent his knees and allowed his body to go over backwards. Somehow a boot heel landed on a sore spot acquired in the earlier fist fight, but otherwise there was no reaction to his landing. Even the riding horses, in the private stable twenty yards away, scarcely altered the pattern of their shifting and mouthing.

He stood up, weaponless, except for the boots. He figured that Katie was either in the bedroom at the rear, the side nearer the smithy; or, failing that, still on the side nearer the smithy and at the front. Somehow, he had to get in touch with her, without disturbing the other sleepers in the house. Easier said than done. But possible, with luck.

Suddenly, it occurred to him that he was right out in the open for anyone to see, if anyone blundered out of doors, or there was a disturbance. He licked his lips, toyed with the idea that he had taken on too much, after all, and ran lightly across to the rear gallery. Up the three steps and onto the boards. His heart thumped. Would the boards creak and give him away? They did not. Just as he was beginning to feel his confidence returning, he heard light footsteps coming from the direction of the bunkhouse.

The unmistakable silhouette of Vic Cardine appeared, watchful as ever, and draped in a dark poncho blanket. From being a lean shadow on one side of the bedroom window, Danny ducked down, stubbed his toes on some old items of horse jewelry, bit his lips to prevent his giving out any sound, and crossed over in a waddling motion to the other side of the window frame.

Cardine slowed up, glanced around in all directions. The mill became a subject of special interest to him, but the hanging rope was thin enough to remain invisible to anyone who was a few yards away. The *segundo* appeared to be wearing moccasins. He trod carefully in an area often used by horses, then slowly skirted the rear gallery. He moved without haste and yet purposefully.

Fortunately, Danny divined the prowler's route and he just had time to drop off the end of the gallery onto the earth. On his knees, he crept forward underneath the boards, and waited. Cardine came nearer and paused almost opposite to the hiding place. Before he moved on again, a tickle in the throat made him emit clearing noises, and then actually cough. Somewhere in the house, there was a movement, albeit a slight one.

Cardine moved on again, rounded the corner of the building and approached a window, half-way down the side. Although crouched and somewhat tensed up, Danny was able to follow his actions. After peering around him, the tall man edged closer to the window.

Suddenly, the window which Danny had negotiated earlier opened at the bottom with a noisy jerk. Out from it came the head and bulky frame of the plump Mexican housekeeper, Fermina.

Cardine already having gone by, it was Danny who quaked almost beneath the weighty frame which actually came out through the window with the aid of a stool and landed on the planking like a collapsed balloon.

Fermina was more formidable at

night than she was in the daytime. She leaned out over the end rail and glanced sharply down the side of the building. Cardine gasped out his guilt.

'*Señor* Cardine, there are folks in this *hacienda* who don't like prowlers in the night. I told you before we don't want no watchdogs. Now, if you don't get yourself away from that young lady's window, *muy pronto*, I will call the boss!'

Cardine stifled a groan. 'It was all in the best interests of the family an' the spread, Fermina, I assure you,' he protested. 'I'm movin' right on, back to bed. I never did have the idea of hangin' around the house at dead of night, I assure you. *Adios. Buenas noches.*'

So saying, he carried on walking, rounded the building and went away in the same direction from which he had arrived. Fermina muttered to herself for nearly a minute, in swift elided Spanish. She moved up and down the gallery, each way, and then cautiously hoisted her bulky body over the window sill and retreated back into her bedroom.

The closing of the window helped Danny to relax. He knew where Katie was now, but at least one person in the house was wide awake. However, he had already taken considerable risk, and not to finish the job at this late stage would have left him with a feeling of frustration. Moreover, he might never know Katie's true view of her situation and his.

Five minutes later, he sprawled forward on hands and knees and gradually worked the creaks out of his cramped legs. His swinging boots kept pace with his crouched body as he went down the side of the house wall to the window and straightened up sufficiently to tap very gently on the pane.

Too much noise would have brought Fermina back into action, but this time there was an instant response. Katie came over to the window and stared out. Danny backed off and removed his hat to give her a clearer view of his face.

By staring intently himself he could make out the surprise on *her* face. He mimed for her to open the window and let him in.

Scarcely thirty seconds had elapsed when the girl decided to comply with his request. She strained to open the window without making a noise. Danny helped. Between them they lost a little perspiration, but it did open.

'I want to talk about quittin' this place,' Danny whispered into her ear, shrouded as it was by long tresses of brown hair. 'Are you game?'

She stayed close enough for him to feel her nodding against him.

'You mean secretly, by night?'

'Sure. As soon as we can be ready. What do you think?'

'You've taken me by surprise, but I think we might make it away. You'll have to come on in for a while, 'cause Cardine was snoopin'.'

'I know. I saw him an' heard him. Can you give me a hand in, so I won't bang on anythin'?'

Two frantic minutes later, feeling quite a bit the worse for wear, Danny straightened up, breathing through his mouth and striving for silence. For the second time within a few hours, Katie threw herself into his arms and this time she felt warmer and softer, and he knew he could soon get the habit of cuddling her close.

'Why, why did you decide suddenly to come for me, Danny?'

'They locked me in the mill, an' that changed everything. I decided as soon as I knew what they'd done to break out. Then I got to thinkin' about you, an' how it would be kind of hard on you if I left without tryin' to help you. So here I am. The odds are still very much against the two of us slippin' away without raisin' the alarm. I don't know how it will be if we disturb Noah. Do you still want to try?'

'Sure, Danny. Give me a minute or two to get some things together, an' to dress, then we'll be off. You don't know how thrillin' it is to have someone on

115

your side, someone to confide in an' to trust.'

They parted company. Danny seated himself gingerly on an upright chair by the door, while Katie hastily slipped out of her nightgown and began to dress herself in clothes for horse-riding. Each was conscious of the other, and for a few seconds after the first sounds, muted footsteps of another night stroller were totally ignored.

Katie stifled a gasp. 'Oh no, it sounds like Cardine again! If he's goin' to hang around he'll spoil everything. What can we do?'

'Is the front door locked?'

'No. Why do you ask?'

'I'll go out that way an' eliminate him!'

'How will you do it, Danny?'

He gave her a brief hug. 'I don't rightly know, but I'll think of something. You concentrate on gettin' ready as quickly as you can. We'll need to collect horses an' make it away without any noise.'

As he talked, Danny found his confidence in the project beginning to wane, but he did not communicate his doubts to Katie. She opened the bedroom door, steered him cautiously through it and accompanied him as far as the front door.

A gentle movement on the hat stand attracted Danny, even in the shadows. His groping hand encountered his own gun belt, and Noah Hickmann's hat. He took the two of them with him, through the front door. Close to the front wall of the house, he strapped on the belt and exchanged Noah's big black stetson for his own grey headgear.

After discarding the grey stetson and the boots which had hung from his neck for so long, he catfooted along the gallery to the end nearer to Katie's bedroom. Cardine, still draped in his poncho, was some fifty feet away. leaning over the paddock rail as though deep in thought.

Danny made it into a wicker chair near the gallery rail. Behind him, the long wooden haft of a digging tool lay against the wall. He touched it with his foot and shifted it so that he could grab it quite quickly. This far, Cardine had noticed nothing, but he showed signs of being restless and of coming nearer, by negotiating Katie's side of the house.

Danny hesitated no longer. He snapped his thumb and fingers two or three times, and beckoned for the night walker to join him. Cardine seemed surprised at first, but he approached the gallery with growing confidence.

'Is that you, Boss?' he murmured, from ten feet away.

Keeping his features hidden under the big hat, Danny nodded and gestured for him to come up to the rail. The big fellow came all the way. It was only in the brief time it took for him to lean over the rail that he began to notice that something was wrong. Danny rose to his feet in one smooth movement, bringing the wooden weapon up from behind in one wild swing until it connected with the side of the snooper's head.

Cardine was still folding up when a second sharp down-blow to the temple sped his flight into unconsciousness. Danny leapt the rail and worked swiftly to truss and gag him, oblivious to what the uneven earth was doing to his feet.

By the time he had slipped his feet into his boots and moved along to the elopement window, Katie was ready to leave. Between them they lowered the frame, and Danny waited until she had joined him, via the front door. She looked two or three sizes bigger, having put on extra garments to facilitate her removal.

Inevitably, there were small noises as they walked out the dun and the piebald mount which Katie usually rode, but as the shoes were muffled no one was attracted to their flight. Fifty yards north of the windmill, Danny boosted his companion into the saddle, and mounted up himself. The feel of the leather under him helped him to shed the tension which had so gripped him as the vital few minutes crawled by.

They had lots of time before dawn, but the Hickmann territory was vast.

8

The line cabin on the eastern boundary of Circle H territory was two and a half miles away. It had been built on larger lines than the average shack, on account of its frequent use as the headquarters of a trail crew preparing a herd for the long journey north to the selling point or to the railway line which linked up with the meat-canning factories in Chicago.

A trail boss and his crew at that very time were some five hundred miles further north driving a herd intended for a rancher in Nebraska.

So this particular line cabin had no specific function in regard to the current requirements of home range and the master, Noah Hickmann. It was, however, occupied. Ringo Hickmann, desperado-at-large and half-brother of Noah, had ridden there by the secret route through the old mine workings, which gave access to Circle H range in a shallow draw well off the beaten track for visitors to the ranch.

The shack was stocked with food, water, bottles of whisky and all manner of other commodities appreciated by ranch workers and others temporarily deprived of the amenities in town.

The horses which had carried the team of bank robbers were hidden in a belt of timber within a furlong. The trip through the tunnels had taken less than a hour; and, out in the open again, not much more than a further sixty minutes.

Until the daylight faded, a watch was kept. The men ate, slaked their thirst and remained in a state of preparedness, just in case the prowling posse blundered onto their hiding place and forced a showdown.

Ringo had been as impatient as the others to shake out the contents of the five money bags and get on with the counting, but he had perforce to show an example until the sun was setting and the chance of a surprise visit was receding.

There was whooping and shrieking as the coins were spilled out onto the broad top of the table, but presently Ringo called for order and the six cock-a-hoop renegades applied themselves to the serious business of counting, like a team of bank tellers at closing time. Hickmann and Halberd wrote down the figures for all of them, and independently cross-checked the totals.

Altogether, in coins and treasury notes they had taken 29,357 dollars and a handful of cents. Those who were not so good at writing, but could read figures were given a chance to check the totalling, and for a while they did so.

Meanwhile, Ringo figured out what their respective cuts were going to be.

'Boys, it looks as if we're goin' to stay lucky, although we shall keep clear of town for a while. I reckon we ought to remove three hundred, fifty-seven dollars away from the main pile. For gambling money.'

No one objected, this far.

'As to the rest, you know as well as I do, an outfit like this has expenses. The Circle H is entitled to a respectable fee for keepin' us under wraps. In fact, there's another matter which might not have occurred to the rest of you. My brother, Noah, had money in the bank, an' he won't relish the idea of us havin' taken it.'

Ringo's face betrayed slight amusement, and the other five animated faces took the chance to relax for a minute or two. The leader waited until they had sobered down again before making his next pronouncement.

'That bein' so, I propose to put aside for Noah the sum of five thousand dollars. That will leave us with twenty four thousand to share between us. Sixes into twenty-four goes exactly four. Four thousand dollars apiece. I hope you'll all be satisfied with the takings from this trip.'

There was a good deal of heated

argument about the shareout, but no actual rebellion. Noah's share seemed a fair one. The others had expected Ringo to demand a double share as the leader. Ringo had thought about such a division, but at the last minute he had decided against it. He thought he might be able to work out some sort of a deal with Noah at a later date. Eventually, all except the gambling money was bagged up again and stacked in the bottom of a strong timber bin normally used for stores. The bin was locked and the card playing began.

The whisky flowed. Hands were won and lost.

Dupont, the former Canadian trapper, dropped out first. His youth had been spent in the wilds. He had no talent for card games. Raich Bardale played well and was fairly lucky, but his intake of whisky spoiled his performance and he lost out next.

Vallance, the short, freckled redhead, had a run of bad luck, and he dropped out. Velasco's heavy-lidded eyes threatened to close throughout the whole of one game. In the following one, his head flopped on the table. That was the end of him.

Jake Halberd of the black-barred brows and lined face had good concentration. He was a hundred or so dollars ahead of Ringo when the leader started to look mean. Jake had known his boss long enough to know when trouble was brewing.

'Ringo, I got to go relieve myself.' He rose to his feet, rocked the table in doing so, and went out, weaving through the bodies and blankets at earth level. On the way in, he remarked: 'Say, Ringo, would you mind if we stopped playin' now? I'm plumb tuckered out, bushed, if you like. What do you say now?'

Ringo yawned hugely and made an effort to focus his bulbous eyes. In that smoke-laden atmosphere it was not an easy task.

'All right. All right, Jake. If you offer

to keep the first watch, I'll pack it in. Okay?'

Jake patted him clumsily on the shoulder, reached for his rifle and took up a position by the window. Ringo put back his head, slung his bootless feet on the table, and immediately went off into a deep sleep.

An hour later, Dupont struggled to his feet to answer a call of nature and found himself nominated to be the keeper of the second watch. Red Vallance had taken over the duty when the eastern sky had turned to grey and was threatening to give the range its first taste of sunlight.

He it was who focussed his narrow-set eyes with great difficulty and perceived what he thought were a pair of apparitions brought on by over-imbibing strong liquor. His big lantern jaw dropped open. His expression was slightly moronic, on account of his short upper lip and the missing front teeth in his upper jaw.

Having blinked several times and

failed to remove the double spectre coming down the draw, he hopped nimbly across the floor keeping his shorter leg out of the way, and stepped into the open air.

He had a rifle in one hand, and a rather battered spyglass in the other. Within a minute he had focussed successfully on the two riders, and knew enough about them to run back indoors and raise the alarm.

He dropped a hand on Ringo's shoulder without avail. Halberd, who was a very light sleeper, even with liquor, opened his eyes sharply and took in the situation.

'Don't disturb him, Red. What is it?'

'Two riders comin' right on across range. They'll either come in here, or pass real close. I *have* to tell Ringo, don't I, Jake?'

'Who are they?' the alert Halberd hissed.

'The heiress girl from the ranch house, I guess, Jake, an' a young fellow who appears to be a stranger. Escortin' her.'

Jake stood up, ran his hands through his hair and stuck his hat on. He gestured for Vallance to rouse the others and himself shook Ringo into wakefulness. The leader's eyes were bloodshot and unfriendly. His mean expression shifted from one man to the other, until they were all nervous under his gaze.

'It's nothin' to panic about, Ringo,' Jake explained. 'Your little heiress girl friend, Karen, appears to have taken it on the lam. She has a ridin' fellow with her. One you might not have seen before. But they've both probably come from the ranch. I saw the galoot, up on the hogsback, purely by chance. He was up there at the same time as Velasco made his reconnaissance.

'They'll be along in five minutes. So, how do you want this affair handlin'?'

There was no lamp shining at the time. The dark shadows of the line cabin were becoming less distinct by the minute, but there was a nice rosy glow in the stove, and the light from it would certainly carry as far as the two riders.

Ringo nipped his already thin, pinched nostrils and appeared to mellow. Halberd, who knew him best, was not taken in.

'The two of 'em seem to be dozin' in the saddle. So why don't some of you boys slip out an' draw a bead on them? It wouldn't do any harm to throw a scare into them, because they might be just a trifle reluctant to tell me what they're up to. All right? Let's go.'

Velasco, Dupont and Vallance responded quickly, slipping out into the open and fanning out with commendable haste. Three Indians could not have carried out the manoeuvre with greater skill.

Two minutes later, Katie's intelligent piebald gelding snickered a time or two, drawing a response from her partner's dun horse.

'Hey, Danny! Wake up, will you? Take stock of things. There's a cabin ahead, an' I have a feelin' it's been occupied through the night!'

Danny blinked himself awake, shook his head for greater effect and removed his hat. Having wiped his forehead with the sleeve of his shirt he rapidly came awake. He was about to ask a question when a sharp instruction came from behind a lone patch of thorny scrub, right ahead.

'All right, hold it, right there! That's close enough! Raise your hands, an' make sure you don't make any smart moves 'cause you're covered!'

The ominous noise of the rifle's mechanism reinforced the initial shock. Danny and Katie both raised their arms, relying on their knees to keep control of their mounts. All they were able to do was encourage their respective horses to side-step a little closer.

'Katie, I have a feelin' these jaspers are belongin' to the gang that robbed the bank. Ringo's boys!'

'Sure enough, Danny. I don't know whether I can ask you to go along followin' my lead, all over again. But Ringo sure is tricky. So it might be best to leave the early exchanges to me. After all, he is Noah's brother, an' he might have wanted to marry the girl I'm supposed to be.'

Dupont had been the one to issue the challenge. Velasco and Vallance, two of the shortest men in the renegade outfit, showed up on either side, rising out of cover with their shoulder weapons ready for action. The latter pair closed in. Dupont relieved Danny of his gun, and stood by watchfully while they dismounted.

Out of the cabin came Ringo, flanked by Jake Halberd and Raich Bardale. Even with her enviable figure smoothed out under a dark poncho, Katie drew the eyes of all concerned.

'I know it's a funny time to come callin', Ringo, but I didn't expect you to receive me with a ring of guns. What goes on?' Katie enquired.

'Just bein' cautious, Miss Karen, that's all. As you say, visitors at dawn are unusual. You ain't by any chance bringin' an urgent message from Noah, are you?'

'No, nothin' like that, Ringo. This here is Wilbur, the man who escorted us two girls all the way from Arkansas. Say hello to Ringo, Wilbur.'

'Howdy, Ringo,' Danny replied, grinning ingenuously, and lowering his hands.

The original trio who had issued the challenge were still alert, but there was no immediate reaction to Danny's boldness. Ringo indicated for them all to go back into the shack. Bardale and Halberd saw to the preparations for breakfast, while the original trio went out to gather firewood.

Seated in the best chair, Ringo fired questions across the hardwood table at the newcomers, who were standing one on either side of the stove.

'Tell me, Karen, did any other visitors arrive at the ranch yesterday?'

Katie nodded. She gave a brief account of the arrival of the posse, recounted all she could remember about the sheriff's questions and only paused when she grew breathless.

133

'Did he ask any questions about me?'

Danny answered. 'Sure, he asked where you were an' your brother gave an evasive answer. The sheriff an' the deputy talked about a palomino horse that knocked over an old woman as the robber chief came away from the bank. The riders left after an hour or so, an' came across the range, so we thought. Did you happen to catch sight of them?'

Ringo, who had gone into himself a little, broodingly forced himself to answer. 'No, they never came near this neck of the woods. So why do two young folks, enjoyin' the hospitality of the Hickmann spread, tiptoe out at dead of night an' head up-range like you two did?'

By this time, the whole of the group was indoors. Bardale, the bulkiest outlaw, was apportioning beans and bacon onto battered plates, while Halberd sorted out the biscuits. All movement seemed to be suspended until the all-important question was answered.

Katie licked her lips, accepted a plate and drew a tall straight-backed chair up to the table. 'We left because I had a feelin' Noah didn't trust me any more, or didn't want me around. It's different when you're not there, Ringo. Wilbur turnin' up like he did seemed to make your brother suspicious. So we decided to slip away, an' take another look at the spot in Greenhorn Gorge where our accident took place. In case there was still a chance we could find that missin' box with the valuables in.'

By this time, everyone was eating. Even the hoggish eater, Bardale, made a good deal less noise than usual. In spite of the food, Danny had the impression that tension was building up in the cabin. He knew he was in the presence of outlaws, but he still had to learn what their attitude towards himself was likely to be.

Ringo plucked a hog's whisker out of a forkful of bacon. This movement drew a lot of attention.

'Wouldn't it have been kinder to take

brother Noah along with you to do the searchin'?'

Katie, who had slipped out of her poncho, shrugged in a rather exaggerated fashion, making several pairs of hostile eyes stare at her bosom. Almost at once, she wished she hadn't made the gesture. Among men with appetites like this crowd showed, she would have done better to keep on her poncho and become overheated.

'Maybe so,' she murmured, 'but I'd gotten so I don't feel altogether comfortable in Noah's company. Besides, he seemed more concerned about you an' your immediate movements than he did about me. An' Wilbur got a funny reception, too. He had a punch-up with your cousin, Vic Cardine, who had made himself our unofficial guard an' escort.'

Ringo nodded and applied himself to his food. The conversation faded out. No one dared raise any other matter until the leader spoke again. Danny and Katie were permitted to leave the table and sit comfortably between the stove and a window. The younger Hickmann joined them.

He began in a jovial mood. 'I'm real glad you came this way, Karen. On account of me an' my ridin' mates are ready to pull out. We've searched for those small stone pinnacles you spoke of before without success, but maybe this time yours an' our luck will change. I think we ought to get started fairly soon, in case brother Noah sends a bunch of his boys along to take you back again. What do you think, Karen?'

Kate-Ellen Armour positively beamed at Ringo, and also attempted to give Danny a special eye glance. 'I believe you think of everything, Ringo,' she enthused. 'Perhaps havin' Wilbur with us will change our luck. I hope so, anyway.'

Ringo turned slowly and favoured Danny with an enigmatic grin.

'Frenchy, go bring up our hosses, why don't you? Take Wilbur with you to help. He looks like he's been around broncs before. Get him to help you with the saddlin', eh?'

With a great effort, Danny maintained a casual attitude. He strolled out with the stocky man who was wearing the fur cap. Side by side, they sauntered down the slope until they came to a hollow in the hillside where the gang's riding horses were either cropping grass or taking their ease.

Danny went towards the roan and the pinto, which were furthest away and pegged out on a long tether. As he bent down to pull out the tethering pin, a hard object hit him very forcibly behind the left ear. Lights flashed in his head, his knees buckled and he stumbled forward, connected with the ground and experienced a sinking sensation for quite a long time.

9

Danny O recovered consciousness rather slowly. The swollen patch behind his left ear throbbed and he had a pain in his head, but otherwise he had not taken much harm, other than in his pride. At no time had he detected any sort of secret glance or intimation pass between Ringo Hickmann and any of his men. He would have gambled that Katie thought also that they had been accepted and that all was well, for the time being.

There was no sign of the blunt instrument which had knocked him out. One thing he knew, it had been weighted with something heavy. That fellow, Frenchy, had surely been a sly mover to get up behind him and hit him with a thrown weapon.

But now what? The 'park' was stripped of animals. One trussed-up riding man, hampered at the wrists and ankles with a linking band of rope keeping his limbs behind him. And, in addition to that, the linking rope was attached to a piece of metal, shaped like a big hairpin and thrust well into the ground.

He was a prisoner in an isolated place. Ringo and his infamous boys had no doubt evacuated, and taken Katie with them. If they had so easily eliminated himself, what might they do to her, a defenceless young woman who could be separated from rediscovered valuables and possibly done to death? Greenhorn Gorge was an isolated little-used tortuous valley, loosely linking three sizeable settlements, including Boot Hill City and Indian Wells. In places, the gorge was very steep and narrow and scarcely accessible, whereas elsewhere it assumed the proportions of a canyon.

As he rolled about on the ground testing the holding pin, Danny asked himself whether Katie would throw in her lot with Ringo, in order to offset a worse fate. He felt that she wouldn't: that her spirit would make her resist his advances, anything permanent which he had in mind, just so long as she had hope.

But where was her hope to come from? So far as he — Danny — knew, he was the only person who knew where she was headed for. Which made him ask himself a few other questions about whether he wanted to feature with Katie again in the future. To his surprise, he was quite positive. His boiling hatred of Ringo, the gang and his present circumstances, and his growing feeling for the girl made him want to fight; to secure his freedom, and to hit back. Free Katie, if he could.

So he started to scheme.

The tethering pin was well into the ground. Ten minutes of contrived rolling on his stomach with his arms and legs held back stretched to fifteen minutes before the pin worked loose. After that his back ached rather badly, due to the pressure he had to use when he managed to get his hands on the metal.

The pin came out, but the tethering rope had suffered not at all. He needed ten minutes' rest before he was able to set off up that punishing slope on his knees with his arms and shoulders still slightly straining backwards.

Three halts for rests on the way up. Eventually, he made it to the shack door which, fortunately, opened easily. A whistle established that his dun gelding had been left behind, but he knew before exploring the saddle that there was no knife in the pockets.

In the shack, he opened the door of the stove, which was still alight and hot, and patiently waited until the metal pin glowed almost red. After that, it was a case of patient hit-and-miss endeavour until the linking rope which held his limbs back was burned through.

He found his knife tossed into a corner, and that facilitated the rest of his work on the bonds. In five minutes, he had recovered his gun and checked over his other equipment. He rested during the time it took to smoke a cigar and drink a cup of coffee. Then he tightened up his saddle, swung into leather and headed away from the fateful cabin. The lock on the wooden box had intrigued him, but he had resisted the temptation to break it open and examine the contents. He was anxious to be on his way, to test out the possible trail signs left by the riding group which had gone eastwards ahead of him. It was hard to believe that the hour of day was no more than eight o'clock.

★ ★ ★

East of regular Circle H range, the terrain was mixed. In places the soil seemed no more than ankle deep over imposing surfaces of rock. At other times, the route was a sandy switchback lightly powdered with dusty soil and loose eroded rocks and boulders.

Danny rode into the sun with his hat brim pulled down to protect his eyes. There was sign to guide him, but not a lot of it, and frequently he rode for twenty or thirty yards without discovering a mark. One of the outlaws' horses had a distinctive groove on a front shoe, and that helped for a time.

An hour had dragged by, and the sign had run out permanently when the loner caught his first glimpse of the regular Boot Hill City to Indian Wells trail. There was scarcely any traffic on it, and no signs of riders resting beside it. The gorge, he knew from earlier conversations, was on the far side. He was making progress, but still quite a bit anxious about Katie and her future.

A conestoga rolled by, travelling north. By the time he was down to trail level the only person in sight was an Indian with an impassive face, who stalked along in moccasins gently leading a pack-horse behind him.

Danny touched his hat and called to him. 'Good day to you, amigo, do you know anything about the gorge? I'm seekin' a place on it where there are distinctive pinnacles of rock. Does that make sense to you?'

The Indian nodded gravely, halted his horse and stepped to one side. His bronzed, wrinkled face remained inscrutable as he peered into the sky beyond the trail. One arm held a cloak about him. The other moved in a horizontal arc between the east and north-east. Presently, he had made up his mind. He pointed in a definite direction for several seconds, then smiled briefly and resumed his journey.

Danny thanked him. He crossed the trail at a walking pace, entered the scrub on the other side and soon came to the conclusion that he was not going to be able to make a descent directly ahead of him. Another furlong confirmed his belief. He rode out onto a big flat rock and stared down into an abyss beneath him.

Greenhorn Gorge was a tortuous snaking valley along a rock fault.

Occasionally, there were glimpses of sparkling waters, running in the very bottom. Water was not always visible, however, and the casual observer rightly judged that the stream ran in and out of rock, at times.

The drop beneath Danny's vantage point was sheer, and several hundred feet. The gap across the top from one rim to another varied considerably. Directly opposite him, it was perhaps three hundred yards.

All up and down the steep sides were signs of plant growth, small animals, and the type of wild birds which thrived in out-of-the-way places. A north American eaglet flew over him, taking in his presence along with that of potential prey.

He used his old spyglass to survey the gorge itself and the meandering track along the near side. No other humans, so far as he could see, were anywhere near his level, or below. Neither could he locate any means of getting down below.

He did, however, see two or three sharp narrowing pinnacles of rock, jutting out from the cliff opposite, not very far below the rim. The Indian's indication had been correct, even if these were not the pinnacles Katie had spoken of. Countless outcrops of varying sizes and heights made it difficult to see if there was a track of sorts, low down, in that section of the gorge. Certainly, if a surrey had overturned on the near side, at the top, its occupants would have been killed, rather than superficially injured.

He had to cross over, and to do that meant a detour. This did not deter him, at all. He knew that wooden bridges spanned the nether regions of the gorge at fairly regular intervals. He also knew that in the last decade no one had thought about their maintainance, and that a stranger, using one for the first time, would do well to tread warily.

Danny chose to detour towards the south. A couple of loops later, he saw

147

the first of the bridges, perhaps fifty feet above the lowest level. He stumbled upon rather than discovered the top of the winding zigzag track which led down the steep scarp to the man-made crossing.

Fifteen minutes later, the dun was across the bridge without mishap and panting a little on the climb up the other side.

About half-way up the other side there was a useful track jutting out from the cliff side, wide enough for two horses to be ridden abreast but scarcely wide enough for a conestoga or a coach. Danny found himself wondering if the surrey with its three occupants had gone along there.

He thought it must have done. He also believed that the real Wilbur Chase had taken risks with his two female charges, in using the gorge track at all. Perhaps it had seemed a much more easy route, if he had joined it south of Boot Hill City.

Hanging foliage and straggling bushes

screened the track from the rim opposite, where he had used his spyglass. The pinnacles he had noticed earlier were scarcely visible as such because he was underneath them, and the angle was difficult for an upward view.

Rounding another tortuous bend, Danny encountered a spot where the edge of the track had crumbled. A miniature landslide had fairly recently endangered the track and anyone upon it. He paused at the spot and looked down, fighting off a touch of vertigo.

Here and there, tiny objects reflected strong sunlight and made him blink. There was evidence above them of bushes being ripped up and a stout tree branch had parted company with an angled bole.

This was an accident spot, but was it the one he was interested in? The bright objects, he decided, might very well be broken glass. Pieces of a shattered mirror, perhaps. He rode on, found a spot where the track was a downgrade and stayed mounted to its lowest point.

There, he parted company with the dun, and used his glass again. The roving telescope showed him items he recognised with mixed feelings. There was another wooden bridge, further south; but even closer, highly placed on the other side of the canyon, was a natural shelf, a hollow in the face of the cliff itself. Movement up there suggested horses, while further down the slope were the unmistakable shapes of scrambling men.

Ringo and his boys had also found the focal spot, although they had detoured northwards. Eagerly, anxiously, Danny probed around, looking for Katie. When he could not see her, he decided that she had been left behind with the horses.

The day was hot; the atmosphere in the gorge was overpowering at times. Danny tried to formulate a plan. He decided to investigate more closely the small, scattered items he had noticed already. He had a little time in hand over the opposition party.

He arrived in the depths, his shirt ringed with perspiration patches. The sparkling objects were, indeed, glass fragments. He also found a smart-looking wheel half-buried in soil and fallen debris. Trapped between two rocks at the lowest level where the stream was no more than a stride wide, he found a leather object.

This discovery pushed all other considerations into the background. It was a wallet of the type used to carry photographs in. He settled back and opened it, wonderingly. Inside were two photos. One showed two girls. Katie and another, in summer dresses. The other girl, almost certainly the real Karen, was round-faced, long-necked and her shoulder-length hair appeared to be fair, rather than dark. It was parted in the middle, over a high forehead and brushed straight downwards. They had their arms about each other's shoulders and appeared to be supremely happy. The second one had been taken about the same time. The girls were separated by a dark complexioned man with narrow eyes, a big nose and a thin mouth. He was attempting a smile, and yet he looked rather grim. He looked to be in his middle forties. Was this the real Wilbur Chase?

Instinct made Danny duck. A long-bladed knife whistled past his head and flew upwards off a rock. He dropped one photo, swivelled swiftly and drew out his Colt, pointing it firmly in the direction of Raich Bardale's navel. The element of surprise had passed from one to the other.

In spite of his bulk and apparent lack of condition, the fleshy outlaw had crept up behind Danny completely unnoticed. Now, he raised his hands in the air, an asinine grin spreading his jowls.

'Naughty, naughty, you shouldn't have moved, should you?'

Danny studied him, noted that his holster was empty. What now? Was it possible to take this fellow up with him to the natural lay-by, where the horses and the girl were, without tackling all the others? At least, Bardale had been away from the rest. And there had been no noise. Probably, the others were still thinking more in terms of the missing box . . .

'All right, lead the way back up that slope. We're headed for the mounts an' the girl. No noise, or I blast you. An' keep away from your partners, eh?'

Bardale chuckled, gustily but quietly. 'Caught lookin' at pictures, were we? What a pity.'

'It'll be a pity for you, Bardale, if you take too many liberties!'

Danny dug him in the back with the muzzle of his Colt, and succeeded in hurting him. The outlaw set off, stepping cautiously, and occasionally dropping a hand to the ground to keep his balance on the slope. Progress was slow, and nerve-racking, but the other outlaws remained out of touch.

Both men were soon breathing hard. At times, Danny was right on the heels of his prisoner. Other times, there was five yards between them. Bardale began to sound as if the climb was too taxing. Although he still had the Colt to hand, Danny was taken by surprise when his prisoner suddenly dived over the top of a rock into a cluster of boulders and pulled a gun from inside his waistband, where it had been all the time.

Danny groaned. Bardale's first bullet flew just wide of his head. At once, Danny hurled himself forward. He did two successive forward rolls through leaves and fern, and succeeded in making it to the nearest rock ahead of him. Bardale fired again. The surprise element was out now. Ringo, his boys, and even Katie, would probably know what was happening.

Moreover, Danny could not see enough of his adversary to get in a telling shot. He decided to take a risk, hurling himself out of cover to a spot where two twisting tree boles afforded cover of some sort. Rising up behind them, he deliberately pumped bullets in among the nest of rocks where Bardale had disappeared. At the fourth shot, there was a reaction, a powerful groan, which could only mean that the outlaw was hit.

No other shots came from him. Danny reloaded his empty chambers with nervous fingers. He walked over, his neck hairs bristling and found the fat man with a new spot on his forehead. Not a neat bullet hole. Something wider than expected, on account of the bullet losing its shape before it ricocheted into the outlaw's head.

The echoes faded. Shouts came from three directions. Ringo and others, enquiring about Bardale's health and getting no response. Clearly, they would now close in upon the spot where the clash had taken place, and having shot the outlaw Danny could expect no quarter.

At least two of the gang were in a position to cut him off before he made it up to the lay-by. Shrugging with frustration, Danny changed his tactics.

It was heavy work hauling Bardale into the open but the body served as a shield while one or two ranging shots flew close. Bardale's corpse slipped from his grasp on one occasion. It was seen to fall to stream level by his comrades, who shouted to one another and decided to concentrate their fire when the fugitive crossed the stream.

Danny heard their shouts, and knew he would be exposed at the critical time. He whistled for the dun, and saw it respond, working its way nervously to the lowest level to meet him. If only he could get there . . .

★ ★ ★

Kate-Ellen Armour knew his fate, too.

She had seen the way in which he started up the slope, presumably to rejoin her while the others were prowling about. Her ankles and wrists were lightly trussed, as Ringo was taking no chances, but she was free to move about without a tether of any kind.

Consequently, from an upright kneeling position at the forward edge of the wide ledge where the riding horses had been left, she had a reasonable view of the developments down below. Her earliest fears were that Danny had been killed in the first flurry of gunfire, but the behaviour of Ringo and the others soon made it clear that a hunt was on: that Danny was very much alive, but striving for survival against odds.

Although her own standing with the outlaws left a lot to be desired she did not hesitate about trying to help lower the odds.

She had no weapon, no way of freeing herself, but the gang had to be distracted somehow. So, close to the edge, she took a chance by attempting to stand upright. Balancing with difficulty, she clearly witnessed the way in which Danny conducted himself.

She caught her breath as the body bounced on a rock and eventually landed in an incongruous sprawling heap across the tiny stream. Bardale.

Bardale's dead body. Danny was out of sight for a while, but she knew where he was because Ringo and the other four probed his position from time to time with bullets which must have gone close. Every time a Colt blasted off Katie flinched, but she knew that as long as the firing kept up Danny must be alive and in with a chance.

One sudden blast almost made her fall over the rim. It also set the riding horses on edge and made them prance about. The girl backed away from the abyss, her mind busy with fleeting thoughts. Ringo was the key to the situation down below. If he could be distracted Danny could get away.

Using the toe of a riding boot, she kicked small stones and soil out of the back wall. The seven horses eyed her suspiciously and moved restlessly, this way and that, on their long tethers. If she didn't do something drastic in the next five minutes, Danny's body might be stretched out alongside Bardale's, because the rock cover was pitifully thin immediately beside the trickling stream.

The ground beneath her feet was soft. She seated herself, drew up her legs and began to kick out small stones. She aimed them for the horses, sliding along and deliberately kicking stones of a useful size. Panic spread among the four-footed beasts. Ringo's big palomino was being crowded towards the brink.

Suddenly the girl screamed three times. The animals milled, and the yellow horse reared up on its hind legs, fighting off the others which were pressuring it. Three horses went one way, and three the other. Too late, the palomino's hind shoes slithered on the brink.

Whinnying in anguish, the big stallion lowered its forelegs, fought for a surer footing and slid agonisingly over the edge, pulling up some fifty feet below the ledge with a thicket helping to break its fall and a tight loop dragging at its neck.

Katie yelled: 'Help! Ringo, somebody

come! There's a rattler up here!'

She thought her lie about a rattle-snake might not be believed by the outlaws, but at least it gave her an excuse of sorts for her peculiar behaviour. For a time, there were more shouts than shots, and her anxiety began to wane. She began to think in depth about the act she was going to put on when Ringo came climbing back up that slope to rescue his favourite riding horse.

* * *

Down below, Danny had been as shaken as any of the others by the screaming and the general commotion crowned by the sight of the big stallion sliding down the formidable slope.

Danny, however, recovered from his surprise quicker than his enemies. He danced down the rest of the slope, taking chances as he aimed his feet for rocks. Soon, he was at the bottom and lying prone beside Bardale. By the time the shooting had resumed he was using the corpse as a shield.

Ringo was the first to shift his attention to the horse's plight. Halberd started back up the slope with him. Velasco, Dupont and Vallance did what they could to harass Danny as he worked his way towards his waiting gelding; but with Bardale's bulky carcase preventing them from getting in a telling shot they soon lost heart and started to scale the other slope to assist Ringo and Jake.

Humping the corpse over the back of his reluctant horse proved quite a task for Danny, but he managed it. Next, he led it to the higher ground and he was ready to move away before the rival outfit had succeeded in getting the stallion back onto the flat.

He was well and truly involved now with the outlaw gang, as well as with the Circle H spread itself. As he headed for Boot Hill City on a roundabout course, his prime concern was for Katie.

Was she hurt, at all, or just frightened? Had there really been a rattlesnake up on the ledge, or had she invented it as an excuse to get the outlaws away from him?

He had a feeling that the plucky girl had worked a trick of some sort, and the further he rode the more convinced he became.

10

Boot Hill City had not known a lot of large-scale villainy for over a decade. It had acquired its name because of the useful wooded mound to the north of the settlement which had started to fill up with coffins rather rapidly in the early days.

Some of the mining projects had been short-lived and the possibility of a railroad running through had caused a boom, followed by a general exodus when it did not materialise. One or two mines still functioned in the area. There was a fair amount of freight traffic through that part of the country, too, and enough farming and ranching to keep most of the original tradesmen in business.

Very little had changed since Danny O rode out in a hurry with his gambling winnings only a few short days ago.

Now, however, he seemed a different person himself. He supposed that he *was* different, coming back as he had with an outlaw's corpse slung across his saddle and an unaccustomed hard expression on his own face.

It was late afternoon, the time of day when siesta takers rouse themselves and finish off the tail end of their day's work. Consequently, there were strollers around the main thoroughfares. Men and women alike paused in their endeavours to stare at the bulky swinging corpse and the grim young man in charge of it.

An undertaker's shingle prompted Danny to ease up and swing out of leather, walking his tired mount across to the hitch rail in front of the funeral parlour and workshop. He knocked on the door, heard a hoarse voice invite him in, and stepped into the gloom of the interior with his hat in his hand.

'Good day to you, mister. I have a bit of unfinished business out here, draped over my saddle. Thought I'd let you know, seein' as how he'll need to be interred fairly soon. Right now, I'm on my way to the marshal's office to give him the first look.'

The undertaker, a bulky man in a black suit and expensive silk hat, cleared his throat, glanced over his clip-on spectacles in the direction of the workshop and massaged a full, trimmed greying beard.

'Hey, Doc, did you hear that? Out front, if you're keen!'

Prentice, the undertaker, slipped a plump friendly arm round Danny's and accompanied him out to the rail, where he scattered one or two nosey townsmen who were hovering too close with the glowing end of his cigar.

'Sure as hell don't need no doctor's certificate to prove he's dead, do he? But the Doc likes to study corpses. Besides he's my brother, you see, an' I like to indulge him. Any special reason why's he's dead?'

Danny nodded. 'He tried a sneak attack on me with a knife, but his throw missed. I was bringin' him up out of Greenhorn Gorge when he sprang away into some rocks an' started pumpin' lead at me. You could say he was unlucky. I couldn't see him from where I was, but I managed to hit him with a ricochet, which explains why his forehead is in a bit of a mess.'

The doctor joined them. A shorter, milder man with a thin face and a drooping black moustache. He was five years younger than his brother who dealt with the dead.

'Weighty, weighty, I'd say,' the medical man commented. 'Not a healthy fellow, eh? Tell me, is he likely to have sufficient money on him to pay for his burial? I ask you because the question seems to embarrass my brother. I'm sure you understand, young fellow, bein' a man of the world.'

Danny finished dusting himself down, and dabbing himself with his bandanna. 'Well, it's possible he has money on him. It's also possible his pocket money came out of the Red River Cattlemen's

Association Bank. The branch in this town!'

The undertaker whistled, and the doctor was so surprised that his big-bowled tobacco pipe fell out of his mouth and scattered its glowing contents in the dirt.

'His name is Bardale, to the best of my knowledge, gents, but if you want to know any more details you'd better come along with me to the peace office, 'cause I'm good an' dry an' I only propose to tell my story once.'

The brothers accepted the offer. They took him to Marshal Tom Stokes, who was in his office alone, trimming down his lush black moustache and sideburns with a small pair of lady's nail scissors. He was also known to keep his finger nails in good trim, although no one in town dared mock him for being dude-like on account of his patched grey stetson. He was probably the only man in the county with small patches over twin bullet holes in the crown of his hat.

He had arrived six months earlier with a notched belt, and a challenging look in his pouched dark eyes which no one so far had put to the test.

Stokes grinned at them in his mirror, showing good teeth and indicated for them to be seated. He shifted his stance so that he could see through the window. The flopped body on the dun's back confirmed the impression he had received by the arrival of the doctor, the undertaker and the stranger.

'I take it the fourth fellow won't be availin' himself of my hospitality, gents. Now, what can I do for you? I take it you want to make a delivery, an' give some information, huh?'

Danny cleared his throat, and began. 'I'm Danny O'Maldon, a travellin' gent. I was in town a day or two ago. Just a few hours before the gang hit the bank, I lit out. I was restin' on top of a ridge west of here when the bank robbers went through ahead of the posse.

'At one time, the posse thought I was one of the gang, blasted off a few rounds at me. I was lucky. Got down offen the heights ahead of them and went to earth on the Circle H, for a spell. I clashed with the bank robbers in a line cabin on ranch territory.

'The girl who was with me, an' me. They treated us badly. Left me trussed up in the cabin, an' took her away with them.'

Marshal Stokes, who had listened spellbound this far, whistled to slow him up, and wagged a long forefinger at him.

'Are you suggestin' there's a link-up between the bank robbers an' the Hickmann ranch, amigo?'

Danny nodded. 'Certainly. The leader of the robbers is Noah Hickmann's half brother, Ringo. Rides a big palomino horse. Takes risks. I went after the young lady they took with them. There was a clash of sorts in the bottom of Greenhorn Gorge.

'I brought a body back with me to prove it. Name of Bardale, I believe. Known among his own kind as Raich

Bardale. You want to take a closer look at him, marshal?'

Stokes shrugged. 'He'll keep a while longer. Carry on talkin' while I have a look through the reward notices.'

The marshal produced notices of varying degrees of freshness from two of his drawers while Danny continued his revelations, facing the professional brothers. He filled them in on a lot of details connected with the gorge, and the reason why Miss Rillwater and others were interested in grubbing about in the bottom of it.

Finally, he pulled out the two photographs which had nearly cost him his life when Bardale jumped him. 'These two girls, an' this fellow, were involved in an accident in a surrey a few weeks back. Down in the gorge. I found these pictures down there. This is the girl I was in touch with.'

The elderly brothers were holding the photos between them. The doctor's eyesight was in better condition for studying close items.

'Yes, yes, I remember, young man. This young woman came along to see me, with her escort, a chap I took to be her husband. This man in the second picture, I think. A sad case. I believe she came out west because she had a slight chest condition, an' the dry air was supposed to improve her. It no doubt would have done, too, if she'd made it to the relations in these parts instead of having an accident.'

Marshal Stokes slowly rose to his feet, holding a faded reward notice in his hand, but his attention was clearly still on what the doctor was saying.

'Pardon me, Doc, but what was it the young lady came to see you about? Was it the chest condition?'

Danny and the undertaker were also very interested in the answer to this question. Dr. Prentice kept them waiting for a few seconds, either weighing his words, or savouring the sensation of having such a keen audience.

'She coughed a bit, but it wasn't that.

In the accident, she'd suffered. Bein' thrown out of a fancy rig like a surrey didn't do her any good. Her bruises an' cuts were shapin' up well, but it was her memory. She couldn't remember clearly why she was in Texas, nor anythin' about the accident. Or who she was with, other than the man who came with her. A case of bad nerves, gents. If the missin' bit of her memory comes back, she may have a bad time, for a while. There ain't no sayin' just how amnesia will go. Not enough known about it, you understand.'

Stokes tapped on his desk top with a big finger ring. 'I saw that young female not more than half an hour ago. She's in town right now, with her man, collectin' groceries an' the like. Maybe you could contact her an' do her a bit of good, Dan. If she saw the picture of that other girl, her friend, it might help her condition.'

Doc Prentice clicked his tongue and shook his head. He counselled Danny to be most careful how he approached the young woman, and not to persist if his enquiries appeared to upset her.

'What are you goin' to do about Ringo Hickmann an' his boys, marshal?' Danny asked pointedly.

Stokes shrugged again. 'I'll do what I can, if the opportunity presents itself. In the meantime, I'll pass to Sheriff Wrangler the information you've given me. This hombre you've brought in appears to be one Fats Bardell. Wanted in the county about a year ago for two robberies an' a suspected killin' by knife. Bardell, Bardale, I wouldn't quibble about his change of name, or what his real name really is. You should be all right for the reward money.'

The promise of five hundred dollars reward money wasn't anything Danny had anticipated. He had simply brought Bardale into town to prove to the peace officers that something was going on which ought to be studied. After promising to write out a description of the other outlaws, Danny departed, leaving the undertaker to transfer the corpse to his premises and see to the stabling of the dun.

The buckboard was fifty yards up the street. The big roan in the shafts was close enough to a water trough not to get too impatient about being kept waiting. A couple of sacks, and several packages on the board and under the seat suggested that most of the shopping had been done.

Danny studied the young woman in the green gown quite keenly. Her hair was long and fair and straight. Under the nipped-in stetson with the turned-down brim her full lips were pursed and her pale blue eyes were sharply focussed on the pages of a novel held open above her knees.

She was young and handsome, scarcely older than Katie Armour and the stillness of her seemed unreal, unnatural.

Feeling that he was intruding, Danny approached her with the two photos. 'Pardon me, miss, but would you be so kind as to take a look at these photographs? I think they would greatly interest you.'

The girl flinched at his voice, dropped the book in her lap, and wrapped the blanket more closely about her legs.

'Who are you?' The question sounded more like a plea than a request for information. Danny moved the first photograph closely above the book. He smiled disarmingly, but she was not able to throw off the feeling of apprehension which gripped her.

'My name is Daniel O'Maldon, I'm a friend of Kate-Ellen Armour. Here she is, in the picture with you an' Wilbur. Do take a look!'

With a hand which shook, she held up the photo with the three of them on. The keen blue eyes made some sense of it, but whatever it meant to her she was troubled.

Danny said: 'Does the name Rillwater mean anything to you? Karen Rillwater?'

Her breathing appeared to tense up.

She coughed sharply a couple of times, before shaking her head, very decidedly.

'No, an' I don't know why it should, young man. I don't know you, and the name of Rillwater means nothing to me, either. I'm waiting for my husband, and I'll thank you not to trouble me any more!'

Karen's face had suddenly reddened. She looked as if she might scream for assistance at any moment. Consequently, Danny backed off with his photographs, touched his hat and permitted her to see that he was going elsewhere.

He knew he had found Karen, but he had also encountered a whole lot more unforeseen trouble.

★ ★ ★

The barber's establishment was run by a man and his son, Mexicans, who were adept at moving a cut-throat razor over a man's chin or in snipping down a cranial thatch which had grown thick enough to prevent a trail rider's hat from sitting properly on his head.

Danny was a little disconsolate when he wandered past, and glanced in at the windows. Two men who looked like dirt farmers had just stepped out, trailing tobacco smoke after them. The young drifter hesitated between having a shave and a haircut, and giving food the top priority. His stomach was empty, and yet he felt he would enjoy his meal a lot more if he was clean. So he wandered into the shop, took the empty chair and allowed the younger of the two barbers to put a towel round his shoulders.

He had checked out a few places, hoping to locate Wilbur Chase, and yet his hopes had been dashed when he found Karen, only to realise that her mind was beyond him. He yawned, asked for a shave and a haircut and nodded without interest to the reflection of the other customer, seated beside him.

Usually, he took the opportunity to daydream when seated in a barber's chair, but his circumstances now were different from any other time he could remember. However, the young man shaved him like he had been born with the skill to shave others.

★　★　★

Wilbur Chase, who had already been shaved, was in the process of having his thick black cranial hair thinned out.

Wilbur's scheming had started months ago. Before he had left Little Creek, he knew that Karen was the heir to a fortune. He was forty-five years old: had served the Rillwaters as a butler, as a clerk in their offices, and also as a driver and guard. At no time did old Rillwater have the impression that he — Wilbur — had ideas beyond his station, that Wilbur thought he had been well used and poorly paid . . .

Wilbur glanced at his reflection in the mirror. He had the dark, narrow eyes which he had inherited from his father, and his mother's hooked nose and thin lips. And yet he had a full head of hair. Only the pouches under his eyes, and the portliness which had crept up on him in the past decade hinted at his real age.

For perhaps the hundredth time since he arrived in the county, he asked himself what his chances were. He had Karen under his personal care; exclusively. Nearly four weeks had gone by, and there had been no sign of Kate-Ellen Armour.

Karen was maybe in for a long spell without the proper use of her memory. He was not keen to carry out the last part of his assignment and take her in her present condition to the Circle H ranch, in case he lost control of her. It might be difficult to make the Hickmanns believe that Karen was married to him, even though Karen believed it herself.

Mr Rillwater had made it amply clear that Karen's future lay with the Hickmanns. Either as the wife of Ringo, the younger brother, or as an unmarried cousin, living with the family on the ranch.

Wilbur had patience; lots of it, but he and his 'bride' were running out of funds, and that was serious! Either they were due for a change of fortune, or their troubles were about to build up.

'Excuse me, I think you may be the person I'm lookin' for.'

The unlined face of the blue-eyed galoot beside him was now almost clear of soap and brown, auburn-tinted bristles. Wilbur stiffened and showed the speaker his best poker expression. The old Mexican flicked short loose hairs away from his neck with a soft, long-haired brush.

'Who do you think I am, stranger?'

'Wilbur Chase from Little Creek, Arkansas. The protector of Karen Rillwater. I spoke to her, up the street, but she didn't take my approaches too well. I think she's still sufferin' after the accident.'

The younger barber washed off Danny's face and thoroughly dried it.

After exchanging glances with his father, he went to work with his scissors and comb.

'Who are you, to be so interested in the affairs of strangers from Arkansas?'

'My name is Daniel O'Maldon. I've come to know Kate-Ellen Armour really well. She's been on the lookout for the two of you for quite a while. If you think I'm not levellin' with you, I can show you the two photographs which I recovered from the bottom of Greenhorn Gorge. When the haircuttin' is over, that is.'

Wilbur nodded. The sort of situation he had dreaded had overtaken him just when he was beginning to feel he was safe on that score.

'Okay, Daniel, get your haircut finished, an' then we'll talk some more, eh? Maybe we could take a drink together, or a meal?'

'Make it both, an' I'm your man,' Danny enthused.

11

Over a substantial meal of beef, vegetables and fruit pie, Danny O and Wilbur Chase gradually learned things about each other.

Wilbur talked freely enough, and yet Danny had the impression that his chatter was guarded, rather than idle. Wilbur talked about the various types of work he had undertaken for the Rillwaters back in Little Creek, but when he came to the more recent events, the journey into Red River County, for instance, he appeared to dry up and look to Danny to take up the conversation.

Both men were hungry, and the food was rapidly taken in. When the fruit pie was almost out of sight, Danny showed Wilbur the two photographs he had found near the scene of the accident.

'All I saw, mark you, were a few

pieces of broken glass, reflectin' the sun, a wheel half buried in scrub an' these two photographs. Didn't get to see the rest of the surrey, at all. Can't say why, except that my investigations were cut short. Still, photos count for a lot, don't they?'

Wilbur took them cautiously and peered at them from a distance, as if he was long-sighted. He sniffed and nodded. 'Are you absolutely certain, Danny, you didn't see anythin' resemblin' a small case, or a box a lady might keep her fancy valuables in?'

Danny shook his head, very decidedly.

'Maybe you ought to leave these photographs with me, Danny. I could show them to Karen when the time is right. She's moody, you see, tortured from inside.'

Danny leaned over quite forcefully and retrieved the pictures back into his custody. 'She's already seen them, Wilbur, an' it didn't do any good. Besides, I'd like to keep them in my possession, because Katie hasn't seen them yet, either.'

Quite perceptibly, Chase's attitude began to change. It was so obvious, in a minute or two, that Danny was quite concerned for him.

'What's with you, Wilbur? Did some of the food disagree with you?'

Chase grinned briefly. 'No, it ain't that, Danny. Not that, at all. It's — well, you see, there's something special between me an' Karen. I can feel it, like a sixth sense, when she needs me an' I have this strong feelin' she's needin' me now. So, I'll have to go. No time for a smoke, or for coffee. Just straighten up, an' out.'

He rose to his feet, dusted himself down, produced the wherewithal to pay the bill and sidled towards the door. Danny pushed his chair back and came to his feet quite quickly. Was Chase trying to be rid of him altogether?

Danny confirmed that there was little chance of Katie getting back with him that day. Chase then appeared to relax a little.

'You could be good for Karen, even if she didn't take to you first off. Why don't you stroll around the town for a while, an' then come on to our place an' stay the night? Everybody in town almost knows the location. Ask for Burro Bob's place through Two Mile Rock.

'An' if we ain't there afore you, go right on in. Make yourself at home, why don't you?'

'You takin' the long route home, or somethin', Wilbur?'

'Not exactly, but Karen likes to picnic, an' pick flowers when she can. So on days like this, we don't try to get back in too much of a hurry, see?'

Chase then cleared his throat a few times, shook hands, murmured a few words to the proprietor, and left the building. Danny shook his head and slumped back in his chair, calling for a cigar along with the coffee.

Chase was nothing if not unpredictable. In fact, in some ways he appeared to have worse problems than the poor young woman with the shattered memory. Danny drew hard on the cigar, soon filling his bit of the room with smoke. He began to think that a certain stroller in the street had gone past two or three times, and that the fellow was glancing in at him significantly, showing more than a modicum of interest. This unlikely theorising began to give Danny the idea that his nerves were on edge.

Perhaps things were piling up on him a bit. After all, he had tangled with outlaws, and killed one of them and only escaped through a bit of good luck . . .

He wondered again about Karen, and the special box which seemed to fascinate her keeper, Wilbur Chase. How safe was the heiress with Wilbur? And how far was she from ever regaining a clear, full memory picture? And what about Katie, that wilful, lissom, scheming young woman who had taken one big chance in her life, and who appeared to be paying dearly for it?

Back at the family ranch, she certainly had a bit of protection, of sorts. But out in the open, with Ringo and his boys on the prowl and eager for loot which couldn't be found, how would she make out now?

Had she the wit, and the luck, to keep off her those vicious men who probably wanted to avenge Raich Bardale's death, and blame her for the accident to the palomino stallion?

Danny shuddered. He ground out the butt of the cigar, which appeared to have gone sour on him. He wanted to be out of doors. His conscience was playing him up again. He should be on the trail now, trying to get Katie away from undesirables who simply wanted to use her!

Why hadn't he informed the local peace officers of her plight? Was it because he thought it was a private problem? His and hers?

One thing became clear, as he left the

restaurant. Katie's fate concerned him a great deal more than the missing valuables. Either he was changing in his outlook, or the brown-haired girl who had plummetted into his life so short a time ago was something very special.

*   *   *

The old bearded limping character named Bob, and the ancient quartet of retired donkeys he used to care for were long gone. Burro Bob was a legend in and around the towns of Red River County. Many men knew where his cabin was located, and many more knew the significance of Two Mile Rock.

However, not many westerners from Boot Hill City, the nearest settlement, were in the habit of visiting the location.

Danny O rode out of the east end of the town, rattled the worn timbers of the bridge which crossed the nearest town point of the gorge and followed a lightly-marked, indistinct track which carried him clear of the gulch area and meandered in a northerly direction.

At times, he found himself wondering if Burro Bob's cabin was anywhere near the spot where he had tangled with the bank robbers, but a few seconds of thought showed him that it was not. He was worrying unduly. The accident spot was probably three or four miles further north than the location of the remote cabin beyond Two Mile Rock.

All sorts of conflicting thoughts tortured his mind. Were Ringo's boys still in the gorge? Was their attention still on the missing loot, or had they decided to concentrate upon *him*, seeing that he had given the slip to both Noah Hickmann and the gang?

His imagination worked upon Katie's possible fate. His face flushed. Frustrated and angry, he passed the time for a while in working out what his revenge could be if Ringo ill-treated the girl.

The gang's biggest setback would involve their losing the loot which they had snatched from the bank. What if a single man located it and removed it without anyone being the wiser? What then?

Two Mile Rock came and went. He allowed the dun to proceed at a steady walking pace on the last leg of the short journey.

What then? The removal of the loot depended upon the intruder knowing where it was hidden. Two places at once sprang to mind. Somewhere in the mine workings area, where the gang had shaken off pursuit, or — alternatively — in the vicinity of the line cabin where Katie and he had been jumped.

Probably, it would be near the cabin: because thieves like to count their ill-gotten gains and work out their shares. Having spent some little time in their company, he could visualise the avaricious greedy look on each of those peculiar faces. For the first time, it occurred to him that Raich Bardale wasn't going to profit by his part in the robbery.

A distant glimpse of the cabin brought his mind back to the present. He cantered the gelding down the gentle slope, entered the lush belt of trees and bushes and noted the depth of the ruts in the path, made by the wheels of the buckboard.

It was a single-level shack made of crude logs on the outside; probably split into two rooms inside, and with a shed built onto the far end and one or two lofts. Off to one side, there was a washing line drooping between a pole in the ground and the branch of an oak tree.

Not far from the tree in question was a well. The sounds below the roller and bucket suggested that it was in full working order.

Danny felt that the cabin was empty, but that someone else was in the vicinity. Accordingly, he wound up the bucket, gave himself a drink of fresh water, and tipped some more into a shallow trough for the dun. Next, he stripped off his saddle and blanket and gave the animal a light rub-down.

All the time he worked, his eyes and ears were busy, but he did not see any signs of the person or persons who had him under observation. As his impatience grew, he moved off casually round to the back of the shack and did a bit of observing from that side. The shed was padlocked and the rear side of the building lacked a back door. However, he was able to peer in through a window and see that the crude wooden furniture and the kitchen utensils were clean.

An indoor clothes line, in addition to the outdoor one, surprised him. A couple of tea towels hung from the two lengths of cord which were rigged about head height from a pulley near the back window to the series of hooks on the inside of the door. A dark brown blanket was draped over the middle section and a part of the table. The blanket looked untidy in comparison with the rest of the interior. Danny saw it, and noted it, and decided he was tired; that he was going to rest, to wait for the late arrival of Karen Rillwater and her unpredictable escort.

After removing one or two items out of his saddle pockets, he settled down, round the back, to smoke and rest.

★　★　★

Karen saw the cropping horse quite early. She pointed it out, panicked a bit and had to be soothed by Wilbur, who said it almost certainly belonged to the young man who was Kate-Ellen's friend, and who was anxious to know them better.

Wilbur abandoned the buckboard near the well and made an effort to control his nerves. His hands were unsteady, but he managed to improve matters, with an effort. In case something had gone wrong, he pulled his revolver clear of the holster and tucked it lightly into his waistbelt.

Stepping towards the door, he called: 'Danny, are you in there?'

Instinct told him to expect a reply, although Danny should not be in a position to make one. Karen grew restless on the seat of the buckboard, and that prompted Chase to do what he had to do. He toyed with the door handle, lifted the latch and stepped forward.

The flash and the noise and the blast were instantaneous. The scorched blanket slipped from the table edge and revealed the long fire-arm, lashed to the woodwork. Wilbur was thrown back. His last remaining strength was used up in clawing the door-frame on either side.

As he sank to the gound, the left side of his chest blasted at point blank range, his glazing eyes encountered those of his intended victim. Danny was staring at him through the glass of the back window.

★　★　★

Karen's scream, seemingly wrenched from the very depths of her being, shattered Danny, who had the bulk of the cabin in front of him. Resting birds took off in all directions. With an effort, Danny shook off the shock and the angry thoughts that Wilbur Chase had intended to kill him by stealth. He ran round the building, called a few soothing words to the disturbed dun, and hurried over to where Karen was rocking herself. Tears escaped through the finely-kept hands which covered her face.

'Come along now, Karen, I'm Kate-Ellen's friend, Danny. You can trust me. Wilbur has had an accident. Why don't you get down off there an' go indoors? You need a drink to brace you.'

The girl glanced briefly at the fallen body, and covered her face again. To facilitate matters, Danny ran over to the shack, hauled Chase's body away from the door and placed his hat over his face. By buttoning the coat he was able to conceal the red mushy mess spreading over the left side of the chest.

This time, he hauled Karen bodily off

the seat and carried her indoors. Breathing hard, he lowered her onto the bottom bunk of the pair against the opposite wall. He asked if they had liquor, received an indeterminate nod and went looking for it. Behind the curtain which screened the half holding the big bed, he found a cabinet with a bottle of brandy in it.

The girl tried to refuse the generous measure he poured for her, but he insisted, applying a cup to her lips and even persisting when some of the fiery liquid ran down her chin. She clenched her teeth, stared sharply at him and shuddered.

He said: 'Danny O, a good friend of Katie! Remember?'

The full lips trembled and the blue eyes, bright with tears, seemed to reveal a normal comprehension, but the girl had only time to nod briefly when the most unexpected interruption put an end to their exchanges.

'Glad to know you, friend! Link Bardale, here. Cousin to the poor innocent galoot you brought into town over your saddle!'

The intruder was a squat figure, less than the average in height. A hunchback with a cylindrical trunk, short thick legs and a head which appeared to be several sizes too large. The soiled grey stetson which appeared to balance on the protruding ears covered cranial hair which was thinning at the forehead. and the crown. With a gun held in each hand, he danced from one boot to the other, flexing his short arms and blowing around his sparse teeth. The big-boned jaw was covered in brown stubble. As he moved, his trouser suspenders altered shape over a coloured checked shirt, hauling on the baggy old levis which threatened to part company.

Danny stood away from Karen. The two of them stared at this apparition and wondered what was likely to happen next. Link Bardale chuckled, the sound seeming to come from deep in his chest. He mimed messages with his guns which were blatantly obvious to understand.

Danny slowly discarded his weapon and raised his hands. Karen started to comply with his instructions to stand up, but her legs buckled under her and she lost consciousness with a mild sigh.

'There's things I need to know, but we'll maybe need the girl's tongue to help us.'

Bardale holstered one gun and tipped a ladle of water over Karen's face and neck.

'See here, Bardale,' Danny murmured, dry-throated. 'That girl lost her memory some weeks ago, in Greenhorn Gorge. There was an accident. A surrey overturned. The dead man was driving it. Since then, she's not been clear in the head. So leave her alone, why don't you?'

'I know. I know what happened in the gorge, mister. But I think you know more than you tell folks, see? More about the missin' loot, more about what happened when Raich died. I know you ain't with Ringo, 'cause he wouldn't have brought Raich back into town like that. He'd have buried him real nice, in a private place on the big ranch!'

Danny half lowered his hands, and was ordered to elevate them again.

'There was an accident out there in the gorge. It's the sort of spot where accidents happen! A stallion, a big palomino belongin' to Ringo slipped down a slope! There was some accidental shootin'. Your cousin, Raich, got in the way of a ricochet. You know how it is with ricochets, don't you, Link? They go any which way, all over the place!'

Link stayed still for a while, blinking at his revolver. 'Poor Raich. He was a good cousin to me. I was useful to him. And to Ringo! I was Ringo's ears in town. He said so, did Ringo. He said so, himself! Ringo wouldn't like Raich dyin'. Besides, I heard tell another story about the way he died. I think you're lyin', mister, an' that ain't nice when it's about Raich, who is dead!'

Bardale started to move about,

working methodically. Having lied without a lot of success, Danny began to perspire. He watched every small move made by his tormentor. Karen sighed and came to her senses, staring so intently that her blue eyes looked as though they might pop out.

She held her hands across her face and eyes, and only peered out of them from time to time. Very speedily, the indoor clothes line was transformed into a hanging rope with a useful noose.

'I ain't so simple, stranger, don't you go thinkin' that. I still think you have interestin' things to tell, otherwise why would that hombre lyin' out there have gone to so much trouble to have you blasted the first time you called? The dead man thought you knew something you didn't want to tell anyone, didn't he?'

Danny's hands had only been lowered for a matter of seconds when his wrists were secured. Next, the noose was lowered over his neck and gently pulled until it was snug to his flesh.

Bardale deftly threw the other end over a beam, and hauled it down.

'Either of you got anythin' you want to tell me?'

Bardale flicked Karen with the end of the rope, still holding Danny secure with the rest of it. She dissolved into tears again, hurting her inside with her convulsions. Suddenly, Danny was on the tip of his toes, working hard to breathe through his restricted neck and feeling his feet begin to go numb inside the boots. The rope was secured, out of the victim's reach. Danny turned sharply, wondering if it was possible that this unfeeling interloper was simply teasing them. Bardale backed off smoothly and retreated as far as the door.

The pattern of Karen's grieving slowed down. Danny found slight ease for the skin of his neck by tilting his head back, but the relief was fleeting. His vision was blurring as Bardale formally departed.

'Adios, folks. I'll be away to talk with Ringo, an' the others. He'll know best what has to be done about Raich. An' he'll no doubt be pleased to know where you are, eh?'

All the way to the place where he had left his mount, the misshapen intruder was cackling almost insanely. His voice seemed very slow to fade. And Danny, who had been trussed before since he made contact with the Hickmanns, began to wonder if his luck had finally left him.

Karen's interest grew slowly. She appeared to be more interested in the corpse beyond the front door than the unfortunate young man teetering on his boot toes on the very brink of death.

12

About every thirty seconds, Danny had to lean forward from the position which gave him greatest ease. His mouth and throat had dried out and his forehead was emitting perspiration like a severed artery losing blood. His hat fell off and rolled towards the only person who could save him.

Karen cowered away from it as if it was a sort of reptile, or a wild animal.

She murmured: 'I've lost my — I've lost Wilbur!'

'You'll have lost me, too, if you don't hurry up an' cut me loose!'

Danny's voice sounded strained, unreal, and it was directed at the resinous underside of the loft. Karen rolled to her feet and ran out, dancing past the spot where the gun had blasted Wilbur. Through the opened door, it was just possible to glimpse her as she knelt beside the corpse and gingerly lifted the coat apart. The blood made her gasp.

While Danny was wondering if he had one or two minutes to live, she lifted the hat off the face and the glazing open eyes seemed to reject her. It was the sightless orbs which made her venture back indoors and stare at Danny from beyond the table and the stove.

Danny was beginning to feel a peculiar sort of drowsiness. He had a sinking feeling; an inclination to believe that it was all unreal. This shack, Karen Rillwater. Wilbur's corpse. And the peculiar will-o'-the-wisp fellow who claimed to be another Bardale. And yet he knew that he was on the brink of death; that he had only sufficient strength left to make one appeal to Karen. If she failed him, he would strangle to death in her presence.

'Katie would have wanted me alive. Katie, your friend. Untie me, you silly girl!'

Eyes popping. His own, not Karen's. *Where was Katie now? Was she having a better time than he was?*

He tried hunching his shoulders, bringing his wrists up and his elbows. Almost, it seemed, of their own volition, the two photographs slipped out of his shirt and fell to the floor. With what amounted to contrariness, Karen moved over and knelt down, staring at them, although his straining boots were no more than a few inches away from her crouched figure.

'You've lost Wilbur, an' you'll see me die, if you don't loosen the rope! Karen!'

His head was expanding and contracting. His eye-balls felt a size too big. Karen fumbled with the rope fastening which held him aloft. The unfastening was too much for her.

'A knife! *Get a knife!*'

She seemed to be doing everything in slow motion. He closed his eyes, used all his willpower with his breathing which was getting out of control. There was a booming noise in his ears which prevented his hearing any small sounds. The booming rose in a crescendo, and then slowly started to fade. Weariness made him rest all his weight on the noose.

His head banged on the floorboards, but the bellows sounds kept up in his head. He had just sufficient strength to shift his head a little, so that his cheek rested on the woodwork and his nose and mouth were both clear to take in air.

$\star \quad \star \quad \star$

He was stretched out on the floor, a folded blanket under his head and another over the lower part of his body. Karen knelt beside him and gently bathed his neck and face with warm water. The skin on his neck felt as if it was on fire, and yet his bandanna had protected him from a really bad noose-burn.

She was different, and it wasn't just

that she had changed her town gown for a man's blue shirt and a pair of tailored levis, either. She was still nervous and her hand shook a little as she ministered to him. The change started with the eyes. Big, round and blue: looking as though they belonged to her again, and challenging, even.

Her lips trembled from time to time, but there was willpower at work, and the emotion which now controlled her suggested that she knew who he was, what he had gone through, and all the shocking details connected with Wilbur Chase's death and the vicious Bardale's visit.

'I'm sorry I took so long to assist you, Danny. I believe I was in the throes of recoverin' my memory. I have this feeling that it's all back there, in my mind, when I want to think back to the accident and everything. I feel so light-headed, I — I can't explain. It's as if my mind had been shackled or something. But, well, as of now, I'm your friend. You've suffered enough through trying to help my friend, Katie.

'Now, I am going to try and pay you back. If you have a mind to be helped.'

Danny grinned and received some water in his mouth. Karen chuckled, and her voice sounded melodious. He allowed her to give him a hand to his feet, and provide coffee for him while he sprawled on a bench beside the table. He was about to get up and look for strangers, but Karen dissuaded him, saying that she had already taken a look all round, through a glass.

'If you feel like it, I'm anxious to hear about this Ringo fellow, an' where Katie is likely to be, right now.'

Danny gestured for her to be seated, opposite. She did, and poured coffee for herself.

'For quite a time, Karen, Katie thought she was the only survivor of the surrey crash. So, she made what was probably the only false move of her life.'

The girl lowered her cup, shook her long straight hair back over her shoulders, and made a shrewd remark.

'Hey, you talk like you are an expert on Kate-Ellen. You must have gotten awful close in a short time. Or shouldn't I have said that?'

A few seconds later, Danny realised that he was probably blushing. Karen was frankly enjoying his embarrassment.

'She masqueraded as you, in front of Noah and Ringo Hickmann. Passed herself off as Karen Rillwater. She never realised what a chance she was taking. Ringo is totally untrustworthy an' self centred. In fact, he robbed a bank in town just a few hours after I slipped away from a certain gamblin' saloon.'

'Was Katie already at the ranch when the bank robbery was taking place?'

'Oh, sure. Ringo had looked her over, decided that he wasn't all that keen on havin' her for a bride. In fact, he was more interested in his criminal endeavours.'

'Poor Katie, she did drop herself in an invidious position,' Karen remarked with feeling.

'Do I take it you've forgiven her for

masqueradin' as yourself?'

Karen bubbled with laughter. 'We were friends, even as small girls. Of course, Katie was always the underdog, family-wise. But there's nothing to forgive, really, Danny. I'd have done the same thing if our rôles had been reversed!'

'I wish I'd known the pair of you in earlier, better times,' Danny said warmly.

Karen clicked her tongue. 'I wish we'd known you earlier, but don't act as though our lives were all over. We've survived the crash, that's the main thing. Whatever happens, I figure on staying in the west. I breathe better, and that's very important. Now, how do we go about freein' Katie, if she's in Ringo's power?'

Danny found himself tensing up again. 'We need manpower. One or two hired guns. I'm not particularly good with firearms, an' the local peace officers ain't likely to do another realistic manhunt without a lot of promptin'. Hired guns need to be paid, an' paid well!'

'I think I may still have the means to buy a bit of manpower, Danny, but why don't we see about the most pressing job? If I'm ever going to be any good out west, I've got to learn how to rough it like the other women.'

So great was the change in Karen from the frightened, withdrawn, cringing young female of a few hours ago that Danny was still in a state of suppressed excitement. There was only one really pressing job about the cabin that he could think of, and that was the burial of Wilbur Chase. Surely, Karen did not intend to participate in the burial?

Her efforts proved that her priorities were the same as his. She had referred to the burial, and she had fully intended to take part. Danny stripped to the waist to dig out the chosen spot at the back of old Burro Bob's cabin.

Karen worked with him for a good ten minutes, until her stamina let her down. He then took her digging tool away from her, and pushed her down on a bench against the shack rear wall and kept her out of the action. Presently, however, she slipped away, and when he was ready for the transfer of the corpse he found that she had roughly stitched a burial bag out of an old woollen blanket.

The actual burial and filling in of the grave took another half hour. Danny saw to the filling in. He then fashioned a crude wooden cross while Karen picked some wild flowers. She was the one who said the prayers and put the finishing touches to the solemn act.

It seemed quite in order when they linked arms to wander back indoors. The day had been a very taxing, somewhat crucial experience for both of them. Clearly, they had to go forward acting together, at least for a time.

Karen tidied up and made a meal of meat, vegetables and tinned beans. Meanwhile, Danny took stock of all the equipment and tools which they had.

Inevitably, the smell of the food titillated his nostrils and he went out of doors to smoke.

There was an hour or two of daylight before sundown, and he found himself wondering how well Karen would be able to sleep. She came out to join him when the meal was almost ready.

'You've done a lot for me already, Danny. Dare I ask you a favour connected with tonight?'

Danny removed the cigar from his mouth and gave her a wry smile.

'Ask away, Karen. I owe you my life, after all. And to some extent my future is tied up with yours. What did you want to ask?'

'I shall always associate this shack with Wilbur an' then I'll get to thinkin' about the way he died. If I get nightmares, maybe my memory will go funny again. Would you take me away? Couldn't we sleep out in the open some place? Anywhere would do.'

'It seems a shame to leave a nice warm shack just when the sun is thinkin' about dippin', but I think we ought to pull out. Just in case that peculiar hombre Bardale comes back in a rush with Ringo an' his boys. So we'll have a good meal, and then off we go.'

★ ★ ★

Nothing happened to interfere with the meal, or to delay their departure. Karen took the reins of the buckboard, with her belongings stacked on the back of it while Danny forked his dun gelding and scouted out ahead.

Just as darkness was draping the scrub-covered foothills to the east of the track between Burro Bob's cabin and Two Mile Rock Danny called a halt. There was no creek in the shallow draw he had chosen, but they had with them an ample supply of water taken from the well at the cabin.

Karen's bedroll was pegged out underneath the buckboard to give her a bit of extra protection from the elements. The shaft horse and the dun were parted and secured on long tethers, one east and one west of the camp site. Danny stacked up a low fire and spread his own roll and saddle on the opposite side to the conveyance.

The girl turned in with biscuits and coffee, while Danny had the same, and further regaled himself with two fingers from Wilbur's half-consumed bottle.

For upwards of an hour they talked. One dwelling on travel details between Little Creek, Arkansas, and the other talking about waywardness, the Hickmanns and Kate-Ellen Armour. They fell asleep within a minute of each other, and none of the sounds of animals or night birds penetrated their dreamless sleep. The daily act of sunrise was well developed when the distinctive clicking of a firearm brought Danny through all the veils of consciousness.

He rolled over into a prone position and faced the buckboard. Karen had already risen. She was fully dressed, leaning against a stunted oak and checking over the firearms which the late Wilbur Chase had brought along with him on the journey. Moreover, it was clear by the way she handled the Colt and the rifle that she had had some training in the use of guns.

Feeling his eyes upon her, Karen straightened up and grinned sheepishly. 'If you're thinkin' of hittin' the owl-hoot trail, Danny, I could maybe help you. I was taught how to ride and use weapons in a very expensive school over in Europe. How would it be if I fired a few practice rounds?'

'You never cease to amaze me, Karen. The things young gentlewomen are taught these days! Sure, go ahead. Amaze me some more.'

He fixed her targets, gave her an occasional piece of advice and ended the session by handing over to her as a gift his small two-shot Derringer pistol. An item thought by some gamblers to be a woman's weapon because it was so small and light.

Over breakfast, they talked again. And when it was over she surprised him yet again by asking him over to examine her green gown. Sewn into it near a seam were six small hard lumps which she passed through his fingers.

'There. Those are diamonds. I forgot about them when my memory gave out. So long as there's a merchant or dealer in Boot Hill City, we shouldn't have any difficulty in raising the money to hire us a small army. If that's what we need. Are you still game, Danny?'

He nodded, rose to his feet and impatiently made ready to move on.

13

The change in Karen Rillwater's general appearance soon became the whisper around town. They talked of how her nervousness had disappeared and how she looked and acted in a positive fashion, more reminiscent of a young man.

Danny ate lunch with her, and tagged along while she acquired more trail rider's clothes, ammunition, and stores in the form of food and other necessities for a small outfit working out of town.

While the girl had her hair done, and purchased items of an intimate nature, Danny chatted with Tom Stokes, the town marshal. As a result, he was introduced to two brothers in their middle fifties, Luke and John Staple. The former ran a jeweller's store and a lawyer's office out of adjoining premises, while his slightly older brother operated from quite close as a freighting agent and removals expert.

Luke Staple exchanged his habitual gold-rimmed spectacles for a jeweller's eye glass which showed him the fine quality of Karen's diamonds and the way in which they had been matched up.

'Could you hold them, and advance the owner, Miss Karen Rillwater, a few hundred dollars for pressin' needs?' Danny asked. 'In a way, she sort of wants grub stakin' you see. There's some unfinished business that got out of hand following a surrey accident in the gorge.'

Staple nodded, almost eagerly. 'I know of Miss Rillwater, and her setback. It wouldn't be any hardship to advance, say, three hundred dollars against these fine stones. Like you suggest, I can hold them. My safe is the best in town. And if she wanted anything in the way of riding stock, my brother, John, is only a few yards away. He's always kept extra riding horses, although he doesn't ride much himself these days.'

Danny signed for the loan, took the money and did a transaction with the freighter. One thing led to another. An hour later, he found himself seated in a private room of a hotel with a mutual friend of Stokes and John Staple.

Jake 'Ace' Cleaver was a man with a fine reputation. Six months previously, he had retired after ten years from his post as a Deputy Federal U.S. Marshal. He was forty-five years of age, six feet tall and twelve stones in weight. Since he retired in the state of Kansas he had done one or two lucrative assignments for private individuals; tasks which required firmness, the use of firearms and considerable nerve.

In Oklahoma, he had taken out eight very persistent cattle thieves who had made a steady living off stolen animals for over three years.

More recently, on the railroad further south, he had tackled a gang of train robbers who had eluded the posses of two counties for eighteen months. At this time, he was resting up in Boot Hill City, having spent a part of his boyhood in that part of the county.

Tom Stokes did the introductions, and Danny launched into an account of his adventures in and around the town, the Circle H and the dreaded gorge. For almost fifteen minutes, there was very little sound in the room, other than the keen young man's voice.

The local marshal then prompted him, and he outlined all he knew of the two girls from Little Creek. Eventually, Cleaver chuckled.

'You ain't tellin' me all this to amuse me, are you, Dan? You want to hire a gun or two to go after this elusive Ringo galoot an' his boys an' free that girl you mentioned, Kate-Ellen Armour.'

'That's about right, Mr Cleaver. Miss Rillwater dearly wants a small team of reliable men to run out these bank robbers. She could offer you a small retainer, an' maybe we could get you a useful fee, if you could rustle up a bit of extra support.'

For almost a minute, Cleaver was silent. His lack of words drew the attention of everyone else to him. He was fair, lean and muscular; clean-shaven, with crow's feet wrinkles crowding his grey eyes at the outer ends. Wearing a white shirt, string tie, a fawn corduroy suit and a grey canvas hat, he looked anything but a private troubleshooter.

Suddenly, he livened up. 'Well now, Danny, boy, it just so happens I'm interested. Moreover, I have at my beck an' call four fine young men who like the sort of challenge you are offerin'. We'll accept a small retainer, and only ask for more if anything goes wrong over the reward money offered this last twenty-four hours by the bank. Accordin' to Tom, here, the President is offerin' one thousand dollars for the apprehension or elimination of the gang, and a further thousand if he gets his funds back.'

Danny found himself suddenly enthusing. Cleaver's smile broadened. He winked at Stokes and John Staple.

'I'm known as Ace, and the names or nicknames of my associates all have to do with the game of cards. Rex King, for instance. Lofty McQueen. Amarillo Jack, an' Slim Spade. So why don't you go and bring along your lady associate while I get my boys? That way we can all get acquainted and formulate our plans.'

Danny immediately rose to his feet and expressed his full agreement. All this time, he had been quietly doubtful of his own abilities with firearms in the anticipated clash, but now the feeling that luck was running his way began to boost his optimism.

★   ★   ★

Meanwhile, Ringo and his boys had backtracked from the treacherous terrain of Greenhorn Gorge. They had returned to the line cabin where their loot was located, and made a big detour across Circle H range to a little-known cabin near the badlands area, west of the main holdings.

Ringo, Jake, Red and Frenchy were playing darts with their crude board fixed to a tree on the shady side of the shack when Velasco, who was on watch, attracted their attention.

The brief whistle from Velasco's vantage point stopped everything and even roused Katie, who was dozing and sunbathing some thirty yards away, in a tree stand.

'Boss, it's our day for visitors, an' it's not your brother. Seein' as how this galoot flashed a mirror, I think it has to be Link. Raich's cousin. He won't be in a good mood, but he will most likely have news for us.'

Ringo, who had lost two successive games with Frenchy as a partner, packed up the darts contest without demur and led the others back to the log cabin. Katie converged with them, covertly watching their faces and wondering if the time was near when she could expect threats to her person.

Velasco went out to meet the rider, and five minutes later Link Bardale was in their midst with his big grey hat tucked under his arm, dancing about between the five of them, looking at the outlaws in turn, then grinning and looking back at Ringo.

Katie pushed a hot mug of coffee into his hands, and his expression changed. She was not sure whether he was hostile towards her or not. Holding the mug away from his face he pulled a familiar white hair ribbon out of his pocket and dangled in front of her.

He had meant to keep it out of her grasp, but Katie moved with such speed that she had snatched it away from him before he could react.

'Why, thank you, Link! I must have dropped it in that other cabin, over the east side!'

Katie forced a smile. She had deliberately left it in the other building, hoping that Danny might find it and know that she was somewhere on Circle H territory. To hold back her hair, she had a length of black silk piping torn from one of the sleeves of her grey, blouse-style shirt.

The handle of the coffee mug grew hot, burned Link's hand and made him concentrate on drinking, which he did with a certain amount of noise. At length, Ringo stopped wondering if the girl had left the ribbon behind deliberately, and prompted the newcomer to converse.

'Sorry about what happened to your cousin, Link. We had a run-in with a young hombre name of Chase. Raich got closest to him, but in the fracas Chase winged Raich with a richochet. It killed him. We don't even have his body to show you.'

The expression of compassion and the open-armed gesture seemed completely out of character on Ringo Hickmann, but his act was to be shortlived.

'I seen Raich. Came into town on the

back of that Chase fellow's ridin' horse. Raich was buried at the cemetery. Not the usual part. Up in the far corner where they put the enemies of society. But I didn't let 'is death go unavenged.'

Link laughed and chuckled, and jumped his entire weight from one foot to the other. The interest of the outlaws quickened. They deliberately refrained from laughing at Link's strange behaviour. Katie, a little further into the background, checked a mild gasp caused by fear. She was anticipating what Link was about to say. On account of Danny's vulnerability, her heart lurched.

The misshapen fellow, savouring his brief spell in the limelight, spilled some coffee, mopped his shirt front with his sleeve and finally gave up drinking. He was more successful with a home-rolled cigarette provided by Frenchy, except that he rapidly filled the atmosphere with smoke.

'I followed 'em out to the cabin. Burro Bob's place.'

Link was seeing it all over again in his mind's eye. It took a fair amount of coaxing to get him to tell the full story. Ringo started, lost patience and gave way to Jake, who did some of the questioning and occasionally deferred to one of the others.

Link described the man who had died. Katie received the news with mixed feelings. It was a greater relief to know that Wilbur was the one who was blasted to death by the gun which he had set up to get rid of over-curious strangers.

Clearly, there had been more to Wilbur and his aspirations than either of the girls had thought. On the protracted journey, neither of them had guessed that he would seek to line his own pockets, given the opportunity. Even as she thought this, Katie blushed, remembering how quickly she had adopted the rôle of her employer's daughter.

While the question and answer session went on, her thoughts roved this way and that, brooding over Karen's loss of memory and what it was likely to mean to her, for the future. She had dearly loved Karen, and only the reasonable certainty that she had died in the accident had made the subterfuge a possibility.

A long mime and gabbled explanation about Karen's weeping and shocked state came to an end when Jake Halberd massaged the creases in his lined face and brought Link back to his earlier statement.

'What did you mean about not lettin' Raich's death go unavenged, Link?'

'I left 'im at full stretch on 'is toes with a noose round 'is neck. The woman weren't up to much. Still in a cryin' fit, she was. So if she didn't snap out of it 'e'd be dead before I got clear of the draw.'

Link mimed himself on tiptoe with a noose around his neck. His performance was startlingly lifelike, and it ensured that no one noticed the sudden pallor which had taken the colour out of Katie's cheeks, or her urgent rush for the door, where she appeared to be in desperate need of fresh air.

'Did I do right to come an' tell you what they were sayin' in town, Ringo?'

'You did, too, Link. That hombre whose neck you stretched, he was sayin' in town that me an' the boys did the bank, right?'

Link nodded, grinned and turned serious again.

'An' you didn't meet anyone on the way here?'

'Not a livin' soul, Ringo.'

Ringo fussed over him, gave him money and sent him back across the ranch acres, with instructions not to be observed by anyone on the Circle H range.

* * *

One hour later, Noah Hickmann himself approached the west boundary line cabin alone, mounted on the box of a farm cart, which contained a fair amount of non-perishable tinned food-stuffs and other stores which could be stacked away in the cabin, or taken away by a group of riders intending to give towns a miss for a while.

Ringo walked out to meet his brother and then came back again; they were seated side by side upon the box. The door of the cabin was open. It was empty. The other outlaws had gone off into a tree stand to laze about and smoke, while Katie went off on foot with a net on a cane handle to try and catch butterflies.

'What did Link Bardale have to say?' Noah asked bluntly.

Ringo quickly recovered from his surprise. He shrugged and grinned.

'All the latest gossip, brother. It seems that Wilbur Chase hombre who came away from the ranch with Karen, also kicked over the traces when we left him. Also, he was sufficiently interested to visit the gorge when we were doin' a bit more searchin'.

'Raich Bardale got near enough to

throw that knife of 'is, but somethin' went wrong. Raich was killed with a ricochet, an' that darned Chase took his body into town for burial.'

Noah spat out a sliver of tobacco, and stared shrewdly at his troublesome kinsman. 'You comin' to the point, Ringo?'

The younger brother frowned, and clenched his jaw muscles.

'Yer, Chase is dead now, but he put it around the town that me an' the boys did the bank robbery. Which ain't nice for you, Noah. I'm real sorry about that. What with you havin' a respectable name to keep up in the district.'

Anger appeared to increase the rancher in size. 'Ringo, I'll spell it out for you! I don't like wanderin' lawmen stickin' their noses into *my* business an' comin' for rides over *my* territory! When this interview is over, you an' yours are goin' on a long trip which will take months, at least. You won't be waitin' for a change in the wind, not even for sundown, right?

'Get the boys to unload these stores, while you an' me go indoors and put the business record straight. I'll have my share of the loot right now, an' don't leave out the Circle H *dinero* which was stolen from the town bank by you-know-who!'

Ringo was slightly shaken by his brother's forthrightness, but he shrugged again, called for assistance, and headed Noah into the shack. He pulled out the special bag of funds from its hiding place under the stone slab base of the stove arrangements and dumped it on the table.

'I have to agree with everythin' you say, Noah. You've been very reasonable. How much did you have in the bank? Five thousand, was it?'

Noah nodded. 'I hope you ain't playin' around none with me, little brother, 'cause all this posse business sure as hell is gettin' me down!'

Ringo gestured, nodded, shrugged and finally convinced Noah that everything was above board.

'What about Karen Rillwater, Ringo?'

'She's with us, big brother, an' we aim to take her along when we go on the long ride you spoke of. As a sort of insurance. That loot we hoped for just ain't goin' to materialise. So, she's just an insurance, see?'

Noah nodded slowly and prepared to withdraw. 'You must be learnin' to use your head, at last, little brother. Insurance, eh? Well, well, life sure is full of surprises. I wonder if she'll like Mexico?'

14

Karen and Jake Cleaver rapidly came to an agreement, but another twenty-four hours were to elapse before the heiress' minor army was ready to make its move.

Danny O, the former federal deputy and his four assistants had an early call at their hotel, and were on their way within an hour of dawn. Karen stayed in her room, because she had met with fairly stiff male opposition when she suggested going along herself on the expedition.

Having apparently agreed with the men's point of view, she had merely done what she could to expedite their final preparations. Fifteen minutes after the men had departed, Karen was called and her breakfast was served in her bedroom a half hour later.

The savoury smell of it titillated her

nostrils. She ate well, and found herself marvelling at the change which had taken place in her since her memory returned and Danny O moved into her life with news of her childhood playmate, Kate-Ellen.

Karen already had a deep-rooted feeling that she was going to spend a lot of her life in Red River County. Moreover, she was sufficiently determined in her immediate motivation to show an entirely different character from the one the Hickmanns were supposed to take into their midst.

Uppermost in her mind was the need to find and free Kate-Ellen. Somehow or another, she had to penetrate into the fastnesses of Circle H territory and learn the truth about Katie and the gang who were holding her. And, it seemed, she had to do it alone.

★ ★ ★

Shortly before nine o'clock in the morning, Karen was riding down to the

236

notorious east boundary line cabin which Danny and Katie had visited with disastrous results.

She had consulted a blacksmith and a couple of veteran locals about the route to take, and how the cabin lay geographically in regard to the home buildings of the ranch, and the southern approach.

The rolling acreage of the Hickmann holdings were impressive at first sight. From the top of the draw where Karen sat her long-legged stockingfoot roan, they seemed endless. A score of longhorns distantly to the north-west munched grass in lush pasture between patches of scrub and occasional outcrops.

She used her spyglass and decided that the cabin she was curious about was not in use. Nevertheless, she approached it with caution.

★　★　★

At just about the same time, former Deputy Federal Marshal Jake 'Ace'

Cleaver was approaching the ranch buildings from the south, as Danny O had done at the beginning of his involvement with the Hickmanns. Ace still had his deputy federal marshal's badge on his person, and he fixed it in place on his lapel before starting across the paddock of the Circle H spread.

On all sides, the hands were busily at work, as if they had been programmed so to do when the stranger was observed. Being quite experienced in the matter of ranching, Cleaver watched them and made up his mind about whether in fact they were truly engaged in worthwhile pressing work, or whether they were merely going through the motions.

Noah, who had been about to leave for his north range on horseback, accompanied by Cardine, delayed his departure and offered the federal officer refreshment; but Cleaver was satisfied by having his big dappled grey horse groomed and receiving the answers to a few questions.

After the pleasantries had been put

out of the way, Cleaver seated himself on the front gallery and stretched himself out to smoke.

The rancher joined him and once again made an effort to seem at ease in the presence of a peace officer.

'Sure, the Circle H is rich in acreage, marshal, an' me an' the wife, we're proud of it, but I'm sure you have some sort of special reason for your visit.'

Cleaver, who had a deep, reasonant voice, chuckled heartily.

'Sure, Mr Hickmann. It's about your brother, Ringo.'

'My half-brother, marshal,' Noah argued quietly. 'He's been attractin' a lot of attention in the last year or two, on account of his wild ways an' unbecomin' attitude to law an' order. What does he have stacked up against him this time?'

This time! Cleaver grinned. 'Well, it could stack up to bank robbery, sir. One of the bank robbers is interred in town. We have a statement from the fellow who brought him in. An' there may be something about abduction, too.'

Noah eyed the growing length of ash on his cigar. 'Abduction?'

'Well, yes. Kidnap, if you like. You'll allow there's a fair amount of circumstantial evidence built up against Ringo. On account of his palomino horse, that fancy hat of his with the coins round the band. An' on account of a piece of paper in the pocket of the dead outlaw, Raich Bardale, namin' Ringo an' four other ridin' friends who go along with him.'

The rancher blew up a thin plume of smoke beyond the brim of his black side-rolled stetson. Inwardly, he was troubled, even though Ringo had left the area. He was not to know that Cleaver's last statement about names on paper was a complete fabrication.

'Is the fellow who brought in the Bardale body around town?'

'He's around, some place, Mr. Hickmann. But what about your half-brother? Where can I locate him?'

'In Mexico, I hope,' Noah answered, with an uneasy chuckle. 'But you were goin' to say something about kidnap, marshal.'

'Oh, yes, I was,' Cleaver acknowledged. 'There's a young woman in town. Her influence has caused the investigation to go on, in regard to the bank business. She was one of a trio up from Arkansas. Involved in an accident in Greenhorn Gorge with a companion an' a man who acted as their escort an' driver — '

'Hey, but that must be Miss Kate-Ellen, the travellin' companion to Karen Rillwater! Am I right?'

Cleaver moved his cigar hand in a slight gesture. 'Oh, well, I guess so. Karen or Katie, or somesuch — '

'But if that's so, marshal,' Noah persisted, cutting in a second time,' you can hardly say that Karen Rillwater has been abducted, kidnapped or whatever, seein' as how she is our distant kin an' she came to these parts with the notion of marryin' Ringo! She ain't here, any more than he is, but that don't make it a kidnap business, no sir!'

Cleaver appeared to think for a long time about Noah's revelations. Eventually, he nodded. 'Well, the lady companion don't see things quite like you do, Mr Hickmann. She thinks her friend may be doin' things under duress, an' knowin' something of Ringo's character I am still inclined to agree with her.

'However I *do* have your assurance that neither Miss Rillwater nor your half-brother is anywhere around on Circle H territory. Don't I?'

'You do, indeed, marshal. I'd take an oath on it. However, if you don't believe me, I could take you on a ride to the northern pastures. We were just about to do that when you arrived.'

Suddenly, Cleaver was on his feet again, and anxious to be away.

'No, that won't be necessary, Mr Hickmann. I have friends waitin' for me a little way to the south. You'd do well not to harbour your brother after this, though, if he should happen to come back. All right?'

Noah acknowledged the warning, shook hands and called for the peace officer's horse. Cleaver mounted up, without haste, and took the southern track.

* * *

Shortly after mid-morning, the quartet of men collected by Ace Cleaver on his travels, refilled their coffee mugs and talked together in a tight group. Danny O was a mere five yards away, and yet he felt like a total stranger, excluded as he was from their intimate gossip.

Cleaver had disciplined them to act as a fighting unit. Each man was an excellent shot both with side arms and shoulder weapons, and they all wore tailored stylish outfits. Their hats were all made of stiff black material with unyielding brims. Their trousers were dark, serviceable and narrow. The upper part of their outfit consisted of a smart cutaway coat with plenty of room for a quick draw.

To further the uniform look, Cleaver had requested that they should all grow a moustache; fairly lush and drooping a little way. They differed, of course, in their hair colouring, and also in the type of horse they rode.

Rex King, the natural leader when Cleaver was away, was forty years of age: a tall, ginger-headed fellow with a pockmarked face. Lofty McQueen was thirty-three and very fair. Amarillo Jack, aged twenty-eight, had perhaps the best growth of moustache. His lush appendage was dark brown in colouring, but he lacked hair on the crown of his head. Where McQueen was on the heavy side, Slim Spade — the youngest — was definitely a lightweight, and his hair colouring was distinctly black.

Danny, who had been listening intently, first noted the distant approach of Cleaver on his dappled grey. He whistled faintly and pointed to the north. At once, the group reacted, cleaning and packing away their mugs, adjusting the twin guns at their waists and squaring off their hats.

To prevent them dirtying their shiny black boots again, Danny kicked out the fire and dealt with the coffee pot.

Cleaver was in a good humour, although he had to report that their quarry was nowhere about. He talked his way through his conversation with Noah Hickmann, gave his impressions of the Circle H and its home buildings and asked for comments. Each and every one of his men had an opinion, but his eyes turned first in the direction of Danny.

The outsider nodded and grinned. 'Ringo Hickmann is bloody-minded, devious and wholly unpredictable, Ace. If he swore an oath to his own brother to head for Mexico with the minimum number of stops on the way, he could break that oath without a moment's hesitation.

'He could head for Arizona, New Mexico, Colorado, or any place else.

Or, he could stay right here, hidden away on this territory, if it suited his purpose. When I first came onto Circle H territory, I was followin' the group of bank robbers, an' just south of here, on the old mine workin's, is where they gave me the slip.

'I'm goin' to have to ask you to take a close look at the minin' area before ridin' off hell for leather in the direction of Mexico. What do you say?'

Cleaver chuckled. He dismounted, slackened off his saddle and rocked it. Danny, unused to his delaying tactics, wondered what was afoot. Presently, Cleaver seemed to have made up his mind. Ignoring Danny, he faced up to each of his men in turn. None of them so much as nodded or shook their heads, but they did answer the leader's challenging gaze with a grin.

'All right, boys, mount up. Danny, here, is goin' to act as our scout, for a while. We tag along behind him. I don't have to tell you to be on the alert, do I?'

Ten minutes later, Danny had skirted

the northern boundary of the mine-working area. No more than two minutes out of the saddle were required to find the special opening in the rock cliff, sheltered by the old canvas screen. One after another, the riders moved into the dark claustrophobic area of the mine tunnels.

Headed by Danny, they followed a route with a fairly firm base underfoot, and where the supporting timber beams were still in place, and largely intact. By this time, the riders were more or less in pairs, Cleaver having moved up to join Danny in the forefront.

From time to time, one or other of them struck a match. After three attempts, at a spot near a fork, Rex King detected a faint current of air. At the same time, a scarcely perceptible sound came from the direction of the draught.

There was life of some sort. It could have been rats, or other rodents, or skulking men. Cleaver signalled for his men to dismount. A family of bats headed through them eerily; as they did so, Cleaver sniffed, and the others knew without being told that he had smelled smoke.

By signs, he ordered Spade and McQueen to drop back and take charge of the horses. Amarillo produced a lamp from his saddle pocket while King scouted a little further ahead. Presently, the latter was back again, having decided that whoever was in the tunnels was not simply a drifter camping out.

There ought to have been signs of lamplight, among other things. Cleaver found an old spade. King lighted the lamp, and Amarillo fixed it on the end of the spade, so that it could be carried quite a useful distance from his body.

The horses shifted uneasily, snickering from time to time. Tension built up as Danny, Cleaver, Amarillo and King went ahead of the others taking the lamp and with their weapons at the ready.

The tunnel made a sharp deviation to the left. Two successive supporting wooden frames, just a yard or two apart, loomed up. A slight rumble ought to have warned the group of what was about to happen. A strong rope, draped round the corner ahead, suddenly hauled an upright prop out of alignment. The opposite post and an overhead beam crashed down, bringing dust, and rock debris with them. The four intruders at once gave ground, jumping this way and that. A portion of the roof fell in and the lamp threatened to go out as Amarillo swung it sideways and banged it against rock.

No one was hurt, although all four had to cough to clear their throats of the dust and it was no longer safe to blunder about, unless the blossoming light from the lamp — which now had a cracked glass — was reasonably close. Cleaver, himself, and Danny O, went back to help the horse minders calm the startled quadrupeds. In the shadowy darkness they were not far from panic. Any sort of shooting at that time might very well have caused a disaster, but no one challenged the determined intruders with firearms.

Amarillo swung up the lamp. The tunnel ahead of them was impassable as far as horses were concerned, but there was room for crawling men to pass between the top of the dust-laden heap and that portion of the ceiling which was still intact. The heads went together.

'Lofty, I want you to join forces with Amarillo an' Slim. Take the animals back to the nearest fork, and try to make your way along another route in this direction. I figure this maze of passages connects up with open Hickmann range within a half-mile.

'I'll take the other boys with me. If the opposition challenges us, we'll take them on. One way or another, we'll be in touch. Make sure they haven't doubled back down that tunnel you're goin' to take. They might have had the notion to get in back of us.'

Danny felt his frame pulsing with excitement. Of late, Katie had not been in the forefront of his mind, but now — as he pulled his rifle out of its scabbard — he wondered if Ringo and his boys had her with them, or if she was a prisoner in some location clear of the mine workings.

The horse minders retreated until only the hollow echo of their shoes on rubble carried to the scene of the downfall. Cleaver edged Danny further back. He then tossed a small boulder through the opening and heard it clatter down beyond. Ears strained, but there was nothing to indicate an ambush around the next turn in the tunnel.

Rex King, who had taken over the lamp, scrambled almost to the top of the heap without worsening the situation, other than by stirring the dust. He waved an arm for the rest to climb and go forward. Mindful that he was supposed to be the scout, Danny went up first, laying flat his Winchester at every move and very much aware of the Colt swinging slightly by his right hip. It occurred to him as he negotiated the narrow gap that the clothing of the professional outfit was likely to suffer more than his own lived-in red shirt, blue bandanna and faded levis. But his heart thumped. If there *was* a sniper up front, a man crawling through the gap was in a bad spot.

Nothing happened. He scrambled down the other side as quietly as possible, tapped a signal for the next man to follow him, and used all his willpower to study the potential ambush spot. With what appeared to be painful slowness, the others, Cleaver and King, cautiously joined him.

Surmising that he himself was the most suspect shot of the three, Danny volunteered to take over holding the lamp. King gave it up with alacrity and Danny took the lead, holding the spade well in front of him.

No one challenged them. The tunnel widened and narrowed, gained height and sometimes lost it. The lamp swung, throwing shadows. Eddying dust and occasional falls of earth kept their nerves on edge. Always there was a change in direction, every few yards.

They had lost count of time when their unsteady footsteps took them into a stretch where the zigzags were narrow. Danny was getting ahead. He stepped to one side, intending to wait for his partners to come up with him.

Distantly, flame lanced the darkness beyond them. A bullet shattered the wooden handle of the spade, not far away from the lamp and the blade. With a sharp gasp, Danny fell back, grabbing at the lamp and managing to grasp it before it shattered. Two more bullets followed, but he had raised the cowl and blown out the light by then.

The echoes worked their way through the diggings with a pulsing, ear-shattering intensity. An angry, excited voice called out to them as the echoes faded.

'Who are you jaspers tresspassin' in the mine territory?'

'An honest man would have found out before creatin' ambushes, friend.

I'm authorised to make contact with you. Only Hickmanns could accuse others of trespassin', I'm thinkin'. Even if I'm wrong about you, you've fired on a man wearin' a badge of a United States peace officer an' something will have to be done about that!'

Cleaver gave him a minute to think about his response, and then whispered for his partners to put up three rifle shots each before advancing. In a stunning cacophony of sound, rifle bullets flew into the darkness ahead, whining, cracking and ricocheting.

Stumbling, kneeling and crawling the trio progressed slowly in the direction of trouble.

15

In fact, Ringo and his party were on the move before Cleaver's disconcerting fusillade made the eastern end of the tunnelling untenable. Vallance and Dupont wanted to stay behind and give the pursuing group a taste of their own medicine, but for once Ringo was thinking clearly, and he dissuaded them.

Five minutes later, they were in the vast wide cavern in the hillside which bordered open range land to the south-east of the Circle H buildings.

Katie was with them, but she did things unwillingly. Her mouth had been secured with a fairly tight gag because she had threatened to call out and draw on the opposition a couple of times. Velasco had his hand bitten before her mouth was secure, and for the scramble clear of the workings, her wrists had been bound, as well.

Suddenly, all the outlaws had an opinion.

'So why don't we get in cover an' pick them off as they come out, Boss?' Frenchy asked, his voice coloured by his Canadian accent.

Clearly, Red and Velasco were keen to partake in such a plan as Frenchy outlined. Jack Halberd kept his eye on the girl and remained silent.

'Because we don't know the strength of the party in there,' Ringo returned bluntly. 'Besides, we might get taken from another angle. They must have arrived on horseback, an' if others come round by the open air route, we could be in trouble.

'We don't head for the west territory on account of we might be intercepted. Even if we weren't, I don't fancy hightailin' it over the badlands to make a getaway. Not from Circle H land, no siree. So, it's back over the east side. If nothin' goes wrong, we cross the gorge, go further east and then detour some other place.

'So fetch the horses, right? And leave the girl to me!'

Halberd gestured towards a shadowy alcove, and Ringo nodded.

Ringo resumed. 'An' as for you, Miss Rillwater. If you think havin' you along with us is goin' to do you any good, don't build up on it! As an heiress, you're a non-event, right?'

Ringo was standing less than yard away, and that smouldering look was building up behind his bulbous eyes, yet Katie felt like defying him. Had she not been gagged, she would have blurted out that she wasn't Karen Rillwater, and that he had been duped all along. Fortunately, she could not betray herself.

Having collected the loot bags from the alcove where they had been hidden, Halberd accosted Ringo, who agreed to give her the freedom of her wrists. To Katie's disgust, she saw that her own lively piebald gelding was to be used as a pack horse for the money-bags.

In spite of herself, she shuddered

inwardly, wondering which of these renegades would ride double with her. They were all wild, but most of all she feared Dupont and the limping red-head, Vallance. Ringo goaded them into mounting up quickly, and it was Halberd who roughly boosted her into the saddle and swung up behind her. The skewbald they shared did not appreciate the double load, but it responded to its master's commands.

Velasco took charge of the pack horse. Ringo led the group up the rising ground, followed by Jake and the little Mexican. Red and Frenchy brought up the rear with their rifles to hand, acting as a rearguard. Two minutes after the fugitives had disappeared over the nearest hillock Danny, Cleaver and King emerged into the vast cavern, and at once stalked the entrance to check on the latest developments.

Five minutes after that, the rest of the group bringing the horses rejoined in the cavern, shouting for information as to what had been happening. Somehow, the exchanges went over Danny's head. All he could think was that Ringo Hickmann and his boys were on the run, and that Katie Armour, the girl who seemed fated to play a big part in his life was probably with them. A whole lot of things could go wrong. And yet, for once, he felt buoyed up, confident. Perhaps it was because he was sided by Ace Cleaver and his thoroughly professional hunters. The real Karen passed through his thoughts. There was a girl — another girl who did not lack courage. He found himself wondering what she was doing with herself, having been rejected in her bid to go along with her own forces into action.

★   ★   ★

The same resourceful young woman, Karen Rillwater, was also keyed up about the alarms and excursions probably taking part on Circle H territory. Since she arrived at the line cabin near the eastern border, no one had been near her.

She had sampled the coffee and the food left there, checked over the other stores and studied the view in all directions. Within a fairly short time she had come to the conclusion that if any sort of a chase developed on the range, it would probably come from the south-west.

Having been around when Danny and Cleaver made their plans, she knew that further west was the spread of buildings, and Ringo and his men were scarcely likely to hole up there. So, she decided, patience would have to be her forte. Furthermore, it would not be wise to be caught by trigger-happy men alone in the cabin. Having come to that decision, she packed all her belongings and one or two items she had borrowed from the cabin, and rode up the slope to westward until she was inside the first stand of timber, scrub and fern.

From that location, she could observe any sort of mounted force coming from the south-west without being immediately noticed herself.

She had kept her self-imposed vigil for over an hour when her nerves began to jump a little. There was no sort of movement visible from the tricky direction, and yet — from earlier experiences — she felt sure that something was developing. She rose to her feet, shifting her weight from one half-boot to the other, and noticed a stunted oak no more than twenty yards back, with a long low beckoning branch facing in the right direction. Her mouth went dry at the thought of climbing, but although her knees knocked a little at first, she was determined to obey her instinct and make the ascent. The smoothness of the lower part of the bole defied her at first, but it did not take long to trim the stockingfoot's blanket, saddle and harness, and to run him underneath the bough.

The roan showed signs of nerves as his agile female rider transferred herself to the branch and gingerly straightened up, with her back to the bole. She had a spyglass in one hand, a Henry rifle in the other and a weighty Colt .45 making one of her hips feel disjointed.

A distant ranging gunshot echoed up the rolling terrain from the southern stretch of grazing land, confirming that her intuition was working well. One lot of riders being pursued by others. Karen's pulse raced. *Who was chasing after who?*

Soon, her full lips spread in a thin line. She was concentrating on the early bunch, and what she saw made it clear that it was the outlaws, seeing as how all the faces were unfamiliar except for that of her frustrated girl friend, Katie. After a second perusal, the keen homely features of Ringo began to look like the studio photograph of him and his half-brother, Noah: a photo which had been sent to Little Creek in order to further the exchanges of information before Karen and the others started out on their journey.

From conversations she had overheard, she recognised by description Frenchy, Red and Velasco, and rightly deduced that the other man — doubling up with Katie — was Jake Halberd. Katie was wriggling about in the saddle and raising general consternation among the riders, who had just been alerted by the ranging rifle shot. Halberd's skewbald was tiring due to its double load, and Katie's squirming about was making its labours intolerable. It side-stepped and showed signs of weariness, nearly fouling the long rope by which Velasco was controlling the piebald pack horse.

Frenchy and Red were still bringing up the rear, and scarcely a moment went by when one or the other was not looking back in the direction of their pursuers.

Frenchy called: 'You want we should head for tree cover an' pick 'em off as they come up the draw, Boss?'

'No, I don't think so, Frenchy. It

would be better if we made it to the cabin an' stood them off there. After all, there's only half a dozen of them. We should do all right, shootin' back from cover. Let's keep it movin'! Jake, if that bitch gives you any trouble from now on, dispose of her! Understand?'

'If you do, they'll gun you all down instead of takin' prisoners!'

Katie's shrill vice carried into the trees, and that was all Karen needed to fire upon this vicious bunch who had misused her friend, Katie, and their ally, Danny. As the distance between them narrowed, the spyglass was no longer needed. She closed it down and stuck it in her belt, concentrating upon a restful stance from which to do her shooting. Distantly, she had seen Danny, Cleaver and his dark-suited team of firearm experts. For herself, she had no fears. Her team were all reliable men, and they would be up with her position in a matter of minutes.

With the bole at her back, she steadied herself. Clearly, the man to knock out first was Halberd, and he was uncomfortably close to Katie; but Karen had the confidence. The target was moving, and yet no one in the group had any notion of her presence.

She licked her lips, panned the gun to keep Halberd in her sights and slowly squeezed the trigger. As it happened, Katie had leaned forward closer to the skewbald's mane as the gun was fired. The crack of the explosion appeared to give the whole of the riding group a severe shock; none of them had anticipated a hostile gun on their flank.

Katie uttered a hoarse cry of alarm, which frightened Karen, as the latter fought to keep her balance and clawed her way back into the saddle of the frisky stockingfoot which fortunately side-stepped and went about, into cover, as the flurry of return shots came from the outlaws.

Jake Halberd, hit fairly in the chest as he raised his left arm, swayed wildly to the right, managed to recover and then swayed out on the near side. He grabbed for Katie's back in order to save himself, but the girl used all her strength to fend him off. As she had the use of her wrists, the dying outlaw was too handicapped to hold on.

He slipped away, sideways, suddenly plummeting towards the ground. His right boot caught in the stirrup and his body dragged, head downwards. His spur raked the sensitive flank of the skewbald, which whinnied in pain, rose on its hind legs and further upset the other horses.

Katie held on, aware that someone was working in her best interests. She dared to guess who it might be. At the same time, she kicked out, loosening the trapped foot and causing the limp form to fall clear.

Goaded and panicked, the skewbald suddenly righted itself clear of the others and went off at a gallop, so that Katie had to hang on with all her strength. Even though it was tired from its double load, it was a powerful horse and all its remaining energies were going into the headlong charge.

Katie kept down over its muscular neck, aware that it was moving away from the rest of the group, and wondering when she might become the target for Ringo's wrath. The seconds sped by. The gap widened. Her gasping breath seemed to be punctuated by the straining gelding's efforts.

The skewbald was heading to pass beyond the cabin by quite a distance. The divergence grew by every stride. The outlaws were shouting now, and there was a staccato exchange of bullets between the two groups. In spite of all efforts, the pursuers had been gaining, which spoke well for Cleaver's men's riding stock.

Out of the corner of her eye, Katie saw that Ringo and his boys were still headed for the cabin and almost there. But his familiar dominating voice changed everything.

'You boys barricade yourselves in an' don't give any quarter! Get that loot under cover an' do what you have to do! Me, I've got unfinished business further on!'

★　★　★

Danny O's line of ride was closer to the trees where Karen had positioned herself than any of the others. He found himself rowelling the dun, a habit which he scarcely ever indulged in. Ahead of him was Katie, just managing to retain her position in the saddle. And after her, exhibiting his usual ruthless determination, went Ringo. Either he was out merely for revenge against the girl, or he had some devilish scheme in mind to use her to his own advantage.

Fleetingly, some unnatural movement from the tree stand distracted Danny. He was not sure whether in fact he had actually seen a figure on horseback or whether his brain was playing him up.

Cleaver called out urgently to him, but he did not register the message. Instead, he waved energetically for the

Cleaver outfit to tackle the men entering the cabin.

Danny hauled out his Winchester and somehow kept his balance. His stomach crawled through fear of falling out of the saddle as he brought it up to his shoulder and aimed it at Ringo's back. Nothing happened, other than his warning the other riders about his presence. He had a feeling that his shot might have gone so far wide as to fly nearer to Katie.

The skewbald took a turn to its left, heading for undulating ground and the timbered area, sparsely clad with tree boles towards the north. Ringo urged his huge palomino after it, and — nearly seventy yards behind — Danny coaxed and bullied his dun into keeping in touch.

It was an urgent, taxing race, but it was not likely to last long. Hickmann rode as if he could lengthen the yellow horse's stride by will power alone. And Danny rode with an urgency he had never in his life felt before. In a couple of minutes they were in the timber. Away behind them, the din of rifles buffeted their ears and echoed through the tree boles with deadly persistence.

The need to avoid boulders and prickly bushes kept the two male riders alert. Here and there a low hanging branch threatened to unseat the unwary. The chase went on for two or three minutes more. It began to seem endless. Danny blanked out his thoughts, fearful of how the uneven pursuit would finish.

* * *

The battle by the cabin was also destined to be short-lived.

Those who had darted inside had little chance to secure their mounts, but Cleaver was far less casual. He put two of his men to run his horses out of sight and did not make his big move until they were all to hand and ready for the climax.

From inside his grey canvas hat he

produced a match. Having waved it briefly to his men, deployed in a wide crescent which amounted to a half-circle, he rasped it on his boot, cupped it in his hand, and applied it to a dynamite stick from which dangled four inches of fuse.

The guns of his disciplined quartet all blasted at once. While the inmates still had their heads down, Ace rose up on one knee and hurled the stick in a wide arc towards the cabin. It fell just over a yard short of the near wall and ricocheted another three feet.

If anyone inside knew of its arrival, they had no chance to do anything about it. Two rifles sounded off by way of reprisal, and then the big explosion. White smoke, puffing and billowing into a distorted circle, tinged with red and bright orange flame. The actual eruption shook the ground, stunned the ears and numbed the senses.

The timbers of the near wall bounced and collapsed in a heap, revealing the interior shambles. Velasco died in there.

Frenchy staggered out with his head bleeding and his arms in the air. He was too stunned to know clearly what he was doing. In fact, he bumped into a tree as the other stricken survivor, Vallance came through the door opening in the leaning wall on hands and knees with a white rag in his hand.

★ ★ ★

The infernal crunch of the explosion had far-reaching effects.

Danny was fleetingly distracted by it, and consequently he was a second or two slow to notice that Ringo had turned the palomino in order to aim his rifle. A feeling of impending doom sent an unwanted tingle up and down the young man's spine. He saw his adversary's rifle as flame briefly showed in the muzzle.

By a miracle, the bullet which should have killed him went between the dun's neck and his own body. As he strove to change direction in order to avoid a second bullet, a section of reins came away, having been severed by the bullet. He had to claw for the saddle horn to keep his balance. During the few sickening seconds of imbalance, he crooked his Winchester under his left arm and fired a shot in desperation.

The crack of the firearm startled the dun, and its immediate reaction luckily helped Danny to get back into control.

He hung onto the dun's mane and wrestled it back on course, Ringo having gone on. '*Keep going, Katie,*' Danny muttered through his clenched teeth.

For a time, the girl had been out of sight. Her full attention had been on speed, whereas Ringo and Danny were blasting off at one another. Salt sweat ran down into the latter's eyes. He blinked it away, and tried hard to concentrate upon his enemy's progress. Something was not quite right. Danny blinked again. The big palomino was acting strangely, behaving as if Ringo had called for slow motion galloping.

Even as the young pursuer gaped, its powerful legs spread out, weaving this way and that, as if it had been doped.

An inkling of the truth penetrated Danny's consciousness as the yellow horse's forelegs gave out and it plunged into the earth, neck and head first. Ringo went over the flailing animal like a huge leaping frog, his arms and legs widespread, but he was sufficiently in command of the situation to turn over in the air and land with his weight on his shoulders.

Scarcely had the outlaw leader landed and bounced when the one setback Danny feared most occurred. A twisting branch, camouflaged by leafy green foliage, came at him like a thrusting pike. A yielding bunch of twigs caught him on the shoulder, showing just sufficient strength to hook him out of the saddle and through the air.

In fact, he had a worse landing than Hickmann, jarring a shoulder and banging the side of his head on a small rock. The blow to the head had the effect of stunning him, making him lose his grip on the remaining leather strap and thereby freeing the dun.

Inert and breathing heavily, Danny did not witness the dun's reaction. It moved forward a few paces, half-heartedly, then, due to tiredness and a lack of instruction, lost momentum and came to a halt, breathing hard and streaming from neck to tail.

* * *

Katie became aware of a change as soon as the pounding shoes of the palomino ceased to din in her ears. No more close rifle shots. No thudding shod hooves. A few seconds went by, during which she admitted to herself that Halberd's big skewbald was in some sort of trouble. Its limping, shifting progress suggested a painful hamstring, or something of the sort.

She permitted the struggling quadruped to ease up and glanced back, taking a long look at what lay behind her. Her senses were so keyed up that she took in most of the scene in a split second. The palomino out on the ground. Ringo on his feet and going back, running and crouching in something akin to a gunman's crouch. Clearly, he was still fighting fit, and he had a good reason to be going the other way.

Danny! Fear jolted her heart, although she did not know Danny was involved in this vindictive breakaway chase. Anything that Ringo managed to do to the other outfit, she had to think was happening to Danny! Hickmann was probably after someone else's cayuse, and that meant that the third rider was unhorsed.

She wanted to shriek, cry out at the top of her lungs and blast apart the big outlaw with some sort of super weapon, as yet uninvented. All she managed was a tortured sigh, as she turned the limping skewbald and started back again. Way back, but not all that far away, there was a riderless horse and a fallen rider.

'Hey Hickmann,' she yelled in an off-key voice, 'it was me you were after! The false heiress from Little Creek! Remember?'

Ringo cackled mercilessly and waved his rifle at her without turning round. He handled it like it was a weightless toy. The gap between the fallen rider, the riderless horse and stalking killer shrank by the second.

* * *

Karen's stockingfoot roan was in better shape than any of the other three, and it was resting, Karen having dismounted as soon as she saw how the two men were unhorsed.

Murder in a man's eyes was something an observer sensed. Karen heard Katie's mounting cry of despair, and knew the girl was on her way back, but she kept her eyes focused more closely on the dun, the outlaw and the fallen man. Ringo was too much in control of himself to make a meal of a simple killing, especially when his enemies had the whip hand. He brought up his rifle and aimed it casually at Danny O's chest.

At that very same time, Karen squeezed the trigger of her Henry rifle which had killed once and not too long ago. Cradled on a tree branch, her aim was assisted. Ringo took a step backward, not intending to, as her bullet ripped into his chest just to the left of his sternum and hit two vital organs.

He jerked about with a foul satanic grimace on his face, as though emphatically denying to God, Satan and everyone on earth that his enemies had finally bested him on Hickmann range. He went down like a man forced to pray, against his wishes, and slumped forward almost at Danny's feet.

Meanwhile, two girls who had grown up together raced towards each other after a separation of several weeks, which both had thought to be a permanent separation.

The pounding continued in Danny's head, but his condition was not all bad. The voices he could hear were both familiar ones and both female. The soft yielding bosom, against which his throbbing head was resting, was that of Katie Armour. She was seated with her back to a tree bole with his head cradled in her arms and a cool damp swab was pressed against his forehead.

Fine sunny highlights sparkled in the long wavy brown hair which seemed to join her face to Danny's. Tiny beads of perspiration beaded her faint freckles and yet he had never seen her more attractive looking. But for one small problem. There were two of her. And two of Karen, who was kneeling a few feet away with her hands on her hips and talking like the most determined eligible female in the west.

Katie noticed his blinking and bent over to kiss him, but Karen went on talking.

' . . . yes, all I have to do is get in touch with Pa. All that money he has stashed away in property, right? I didn't really bring a lot of money or valuables with me. I was to get in touch just as soon as I knew what I wanted to do. You know, I've made up my mind. This very afternoon.

'I'm goin' to make things hot for Noah Hickmann. Lean on him. Maybe have Jake Cleaver harass him a bit. I aim to make Noah sell out his holdings to me. Unless I hear of a better patch of land, better stocked with animals, that is. You approve?

'Wilbur isn't with us any more, but you an' me, Katie, we're going to dig ourselves in here, in this neck of the woods, make a new life for ourselves, an' put *our* sort of people about us. That there young Danny O'Maldon you're holding, he doesn't know it, but his drifting days are over.

'Make sure you have him hogtied by the time he regains his senses, even if you have to marry the jasper! We'll need him to ramrod our new place, or at least to behave like the man about the house; so help me, we'll need to have him around us, one way or another!'

The thumping in Danny's head was slowly fading. Relief and the knowledge that he was hearing a truly worthwhile future being mapped out for him made him relax. In spite of everything, he began to see the funny side of the present situation.

Katie knew the mild jerking movement meant he was laughing, but she was enjoying the situation, so she did not remark on it. Presently, Karen stood up and sighed.

'Here comes Cleaver now, grinning like he's grabbed all the loot an' made a clean sweep. I'll go along and meet him.'

As her footsteps faded, Danny opened his eyes with great care. To his great relief he saw only one of Katie, instead of two. They kissed and examined one another's faces from very close up.

'Katie, I'm gettin' so I worry about you all the time you're out of sight.'

The girl gasped. 'Land's sakes, Danny, I have exactly the same sort of trouble. I guess there's only one way to cure ourselves. Stay close, till it wears off.'

'Hm, maybe that won't ever happen!'

Slowly, and with great deliberation, they helped one another to stand upright and waited hand in hand for company.

THE END